4

THE ADVENTURES

TRAVELS
IN
HONG KONG

OF THE

KERRIGAN KIDS

NINE-STORY
PAGODAS & DOUBLE-
DECKER BUSES

THE ADVENTURES OF THE

4

TRAVELS IN HONG KONG

OF THE

KERRIGAN KIDS

NINE-STORY PAGODAS & DOUBLE-DECKER BUSES

GILBERT MORRIS

MOODY PRESS
CHICAGO

© 2001 by
GILBERT MORRIS

Library of Congress Cataloging-in-Publication Data

Morris, Gilbert
    Nine-story pagodas and double-decker buses : travel in
Hong Kong / Gilbert Morris.
        p. cm. -- (Adventures of the Kerrigan kids ; #4)
    Sequel to: Kangaroos and the outback: travel in Australia.
    Summary: During the Kerrigan family's trip to Hong Kong,
  Duffy and her adopted siblings befriend and share their Christian faith with two orphaned children who have come to live
  with their Chinese grandparents.
    ISBN: 0-8024-1581-4
    [1. Orphans--Fiction. 2. Brothers and sisters--Fiction.
  3. Adoption--Fiction. 4. Interracial adoption--Fiction.
  5. Sincle-parent families--Fiction. 6. Hong Kong (China)--
  Fiction. 7. Christian life--Fiction.] I. Title

PZ7.M8279 Ni 2001
[Fic]--dc21

                                          00-049016

1 3 5 7 9 10 8 6 4 2

Printed in the United States of America

CONTENTS

1. All Aboard 7
2. Hong Kong 19
3. Too Many People 27
4. A Meal to Remember 41
5. Two Sad Kids 47
6. Mr. and Mrs. Li 57
7. The Zoo 65
8. The Church 75
9. Trouble for Juan 89
10. A Night at the Li House 101
11. The Shopping Trip 109
12. Heading Home 117

ALL
ABOARD

The four Kerrigan kids sat in a row listening to their Sunday school teacher. They usually liked to hear Miss Smith's interesting stories from the Bible.

But the lesson for this morning was the story of the Good Samaritan, and Juan Kerrigan, age ten, thought he knew it well. He leaned over and whispered to Seth, "I could teach this lesson as good as she could."

Juan had been born in Mexico and was left at the door of an orphanage run by missionaries. Seth had been born in Nigeria and had spent the first few years of his life in British schools, so he spoke with a crisp, British accent.

Seth whispered back, "You always think you can do everything, Juan."

"Well, I can!"

Their sister Duffy, age twelve, was sitting on Juan's other side. She dug an elbow into his ribs. "Will you be quiet? I want to hear what Miss Smith is saying!"

Duffy had red hair and was leggy just like her father. She had been the Kerrigans' only child, so they adopted Juan and Seth and Pearl, a pretty Asian girl who had coal black hair and almond-shaped eyes.

"And so what lesson is God teaching us from the story of the Good Samaritan?" Miss Smith asked. "Pearl, what do you think?"

Pearl thought for a moment and then said, "It teaches us that we need to help people who are in trouble."

"That's one lesson," Miss Smith agreed.

"And more than that," Duffy said quickly, "the Good Samaritan was a different nationality from the man that was hurt. So God wants us to be good even to people who are different from us."

"And that is certainly true, Duffy."

"I think a rifle's the best idea," Juan piped up, grinning. "If that guy had carried one, he could have shot all those bandits, and that would have settled that."

Miss Smith ignored Juan and looked at her watch. "It's almost time to go. I need to step out of the class for just a minute. You'll be very still, won't you, and then we'll go out to the church service."

As soon as the door closed, Juan said, "Aw, if that guy had had an AK-47 attack rifle, he could have cleaned up on the whole crew of robbers."

"Why don't you be quiet, Juan! You just like to show off." Ralph Carmody was the largest boy in the class. He reached from behind and rapped Juan on the head. "And you talk too much!"

As soon as Juan felt the sharp blow to the back of his head, he leaped up and over the back of his chair, upsetting it. He landed on Ralph Carmody, and the two fell to the floor between the rows of seats.

"Hey, get off me!" Ralph yelled.

Everyone began to talk then, but it was Duffy who pulled Juan off Ralph by the hair of his head.

"Ow, you're pulling my hair out!"

"Well, leave him alone! This is Sunday school."

"You might look pretty good baldheaded," Seth said.

The boys had just set the chairs straight when Miss Smith came back to dismiss them. She took one look and said, "Is something wrong?"

"Not now, Miss Smith," Duffy said quickly. "Now come on, Juan, let's go in to church."

The Kerrigan kids found their father sitting at his usual place. He was a tall, lean man. He had warm, brown eyes and tousled brown hair that would never stay combed. Even now he ran his hands through it and messed it up even worse.

"Dad, stop messing your hair up," Juan said.

Their dad taught Sunday school sometimes, but his work took him away a great deal of the time. He was a photographer, and his journeys took him to many interesting spots in the world. After Mrs. Kerrigan died, he'd begun taking the children along with him. Already he had taken them to Africa, England, and Australia.

The Kerrigan kids joined in the church service. They could all sing well. And although their dad could barely carry a tune, he seemed pleased with their musical ability. Duffy played the piano, Seth the bass guitar, Juan the lead guitar, and Pearl was learning to play the drums.

After church, the pastor greeted them at the door. "I understand you're leaving for another trip, Brother Kerrigan."

"That's right, pastor. We'll be going to Hong Kong this time."

"It must be nice to get to travel like that—and get paid for it."

"Yeah, and he's got us to take care of him," Juan piped up. Then he said, "Do you know what's the strongest day in the week?"

"No, I don't believe I do, Juan," the pastor said. "What is the strongest day in the week?"

"Sunday! The rest are all weak days." Juan laughed loudly. "Don't you get it? Weak days. W-e-a-k. Weak."

"Ah, that's a good one, Juan. I'll have to re-member that."

"Come on, Juan," Mr. Kerrigan said. "I don't think the pastor needs any more of your terrible jokes."

They proceeded to the car, and as soon as they got in, Seth began talking about the Hong Kong trip. "It'll be like going home for you, Pearl."

"I still remember some of it," Pearl said. "And some Chinese too."

Their father smiled. "This time we'll have our own interpreter along with us."

"You know," Duffy said, "every trip we've made has been just great." She slid over nearer to her dad, for she liked to sit very close to him. "I think my favorite place was England."

"Not me," Seth said. "I liked Africa the best. All those lions and zebras."

"I think I liked Australia the best," Pearl said. "The people there were so nice and friendly."

The family talked about their trips to foreign lands until they got home.

"All right. Time to start packing," Mr. Kerrigan said the next morning. "Do a good job, because I'll come around to inspect your bags. The last time, Juan, you tried to carry a bunch of winter clothes all the way to Australia."

"I thought it might snow," Juan said cheerfully. "It was winter here."

"But summer there," Mr. Kerrigan pointed out.

Seth and Juan went to their room, and Juan took down two suitcases. He threw them onto the bed. As soon as he opened them, he began tossing in clothes, not bothering to fold anything.

Seth, on the other hand, folded every garment, even his socks, very carefully. He glanced over once, saw the mess Juan was making, and shook his head but said nothing.

Juan must have seen the glance. He said, "You don't need to be so careful. You'll just have to unpack it again when we get to Hong Kong."

"I like to do things neatly, and you should try to be neater yourself."

"I'm a neat guy." Juan picked up a football and crammed it into his bag, then closed the lid. It made a huge lump.

"You can't carry that thing all the way to Hong Kong!"

"Sure I can. How would we play football if we didn't have a football?"

Seth groaned in disgust. "Well, at least let the air out of it."

"Oh no. It's OK."

In the girls' bedroom, Duffy and Pearl had their luggage on the bed. Both had suitcases with hangers in them, and they were carefully hanging up each dress.

Duffy put in a lime green dress, then said, "No

matter how careful I am, my clothes always get wrinkled."

"We can iron them when we get there," Pearl said. She then laid out several books.

Duffy said, "You don't think you're going to have time to *read,* do you?"

"Oh, at least on the airplane."

"They always show a movie on the plane. Don't you remember?"

"I didn't like the movies they showed when we went to Australia. I'd rather take a book."

When the girls tired of packing, they started trying on clothes and modeling for one another.

And then the door opened, and Juan peered in. His eyes lit up, and he walked through the doorway pretending to walk like a girl. "Oh, Seth," he called in a high voice, "how do I look in this pink dress and these white shoes?" He put one hand up to his hair and pretended to fix it as a girl might.

But Juan was not the only Kerrigan that had somewhat of a temper. With one motion Duffy turned and threw one of her Keds. It struck Juan right on the forehead.

"Hey, what are you doing?" Juan gathered up the shoe and threw it back. Duffy began showering him with shoes, and he began throwing them back at her.

The two were both taking hits when all of a sudden Mr. Kerrigan stepped in. "What do you two think you are doing?"

Juan gaped at his father for a moment. "Oh, nothing, Dad. We're just fooling around."

"Well, you've fooled around enough. Now pack your clothes."

"I'm already packed!" Juan protested.

"Is that so? Let me see."

They all walked down to the boys' room, and Juan waved to his suitcases. "See. All closed and ready to go."

"What's this big lump?"

"That's his dumb football, Dad. I tried to get him not to take it or at least to let the air out."

"You won't need a football in Hong Kong. We'll be too busy. Take your math book. You can play with that."

Juan frowned. He knew he was very bad at math. "Aw, Dad, this is a vacation. I don't want to work."

"It's not a vacation for me. It's going to be hard work getting all those pictures. You kids are going to have to entertain yourselves some of the time. It's not a vacation from school for you, either. Take whatever books you'll need so you don't get behind while we're away."

"I'll take my English book," Duffy said. "You can help me with it, Dad. You're real good at English."

"Sure I will. And all of us will help Juan. He thinks two plus two is six."

"I do not!" Juan flushed. "I'll show you. I'm going to make an A in math."

"Good for you, son. I'm for that."

The plane was huge, as all planes were that flew over the Pacific Ocean.

The children had slept all night during the flight, and there were still many hours to go.

Mr. Kerrigan sat in an aisle seat with maps out in front of him. He was studying them intently.

He looked up at Pearl, who slid over to sit beside him. "Hong Kong is a big city."

"I remember there were lots of people there."

"Well, now you'll get to see again the place where you were born."

"That'll be fun," Pearl said. "Show me some of the places on the map where you're going to take pictures."

The plane droned on, and after a while the movie came on. It was a film about a giant lizard that attacked some skyscrapers.

None of the kids had seen it, and Juan thought it was great fun.

"That's quite a lizard," he said.

But Seth shook his head. "It looks so phony. It's a real bad movie."

"Ah, you don't like any good movies!"

"I don't think there are many," Seth said gloomily.

After the movie was over, they tried listening to music over their earphones. Duffy liked the country western music best. Juan liked anything noisy, and Pearl liked the easy listening music. Seth found some South American music, and he liked the beat of that very much. He sat moving from side to side, keeping time. "I wish I had my guitar here," he said. "I could play along with it."

After a while, Duffy went to get a drink of water. According to the flight attendant, it was still an hour until meal time. As she came back, she noticed two children sitting alone two rows ahead of them. They were Chinese, like Pearl, she thought. She was curious, for she could hear them talking, and they were speaking English.

Duffy was not a shy young lady, and she stopped beside them. "Hi," she said. "My name is Duffy Kerrigan."

"I am Saun Li," the girl said. "And this is my brother, Ping."

"You're going to Hong Kong?" Duffy asked.

"Yes, we are. Are you going also?"

"Our whole family is going there."

"Is that your family back there, two rows back?" Saun asked.

"Yes, it is."

"But the small girl is Chinese."

"Well, my two brothers and my sister were all adopted, you see. Would you like to meet them?"

The two looked rather shy, so Duffy said, "You'll like them, I'm sure. I'll go get them."

She went back to where the others were sitting

and said, "There are two kids up there going to Hong Kong. Come on. You can meet them."

Maybe by this time Seth and Juan and Pearl were getting bored, for they got up at once to meet the two Oriental children. "This is Ping"—Duffy indicated the boy—"and this is Saun." The Li children said hello very timidly.

Juan said, "Are you from Hong Kong?"

"No," Saun said. She seemed to be the speaker for the two. "We lived in Los Angeles, but now we're going to Hong Kong to live with our grandparents."

"Why are you doing that?" Juan asked.

Tears came into the boy's eyes. "Our mother and father died in a car wreck. We have no family in America now."

Saun's eyes were also sad.

Duffy wanted to comfort the children. "You'll have a good home with your grandparents. Maybe we'll see you while we're in Hong Kong."

The Kerrigans got on very well with the Li children. After supper was brought, they went up to talk with them again instead of staying with their father. He was busy with his maps anyway. Ping warmed up to Seth, who treated him like a younger brother. Saun got along well with both girls. Duffy soon felt herself to be good friends with the Chinese children.

When they finally were ready to go back to their seats, Duffy said, "You're going to like it in

Hong Kong. From what all the books say, it's one of the most exciting cities in the world!"

HONG KONG

"All passengers, please fasten your seatbelts."
The voice of the pilot came over the loud-speaker, and the Kerrigan kids began scrambling back to their seats. During their long flight, Duffy and the others had stayed in the aisle about as much as they had stayed in their seats. They had made regular and unnecessary trips to get water and many trips to the restroom. The meals, Duffy thought, had been great. In fact, she felt like a stuffed sausage by the time she heard the pilot's warning.

"What time is it?" Juan asked his father.

Mr. Kerrigan looked at his watch. "About six o'clock," he said. "It's just about dawn."

"What time is it back home?" Pearl wanted to know.

"About three in the afternoon," Juan said.

Duffy looked at him with disgust. "You don't know that! You just made it up."

"No, I didn't. I figured it out!" Juan protested.

Duffy ignored him, for Juan never admitted ignorance on any subject. She watched out the window as the huge plane came down, and it was a breathtaking sight.

Her father said, "There it is—Hong Kong International Airport! This place is called Chek Lap Tok."

The plane lowered, and now it skimmed between buildings. It seemed to Duffy a very dangerous place to put an airport.

And then the plane touched down on a narrow runway. Water stretched out on either side.

"Hey, this runway goes out into the ocean!" Juan cried out with alarm. "We're all going to drown!"

"I'm sure we won't, Juan." Mr. Kerrigan grinned. "They do this every day. They even call this the 'world's favorite airport.'"

Pearl held her breath and closed her eyes, but Duffy watched. The plane rolled to a stop just before they got to the end of the runway.

"Time to get off," Mr. Kerrigan said cheerfully, once the plane reached the terminal.

"I always hate the end of these flights," Seth muttered. "Trying to find your baggage and going through customs."

"That's just a way of life for travelers. Let's go," his dad urged.

It took some time for the passengers to get off the plane, for there were several hundred of them. Most had carried on small bags, but the larger bags had been put in the cargo hold underneath.

"We'll get our baggage first."

They found their way to the baggage claim area. Duffy watched for them to come rolling around on the circular track.

Juan spotted his purple and orange bags first and cried, "There they are! Those are mine."

"They're so tacky looking," Duffy said with disgust.

"They've got no class. No dignity," Seth said. "Now you take *my* bag. It's nice and brown."

But it was true that Juan found his bags much easier than the others did. Finally they had all of their suitcases and loaded them onto a small cart. Mr. Kerrigan pushed it until they came to customs. This took considerable time. Everyone had to go through and talk to the customs inspector, a moon-faced, Chinese lady who asked them if they were coming on business or on a vacation. She finally stamped the Kerrigans' passports and checked them on through.

"Do you know where to go now, Dad?" Duffy asked.

"Yes, the next thing is to get some Hong Kong money."

"It'd be nice if everybody used the same kind of money, wouldn't it?" Pearl said.

"Sure would, honey, but that's not the way it is."

They found the information desk and then made their way to Buffer Hall, where Mr. Kerrigan changed some of their American money for Hong Kong dollars. Then the family started for the exit where the transportation to Hong Kong Island could be found.

As they walked along, Duffy was stunned by the crowds of people. It was a very large airport, and she saw not only Westerners and Chinese but also Indians with turbans and Muslim women with black veils over their faces.

"Oh, look," Pearl cried. "There's Ping and Saun."

Then Duffy too saw the Li children. They were standing alone, looking down at a piece of paper.

"They look worried. Let's go see if they need help," Mr. Kerrigan said.

"Why, hello there, youngsters," he said to them. "Was somebody supposed to meet you?"

"Yes, but they're not here."

"Something must have gone wrong," Duffy said.

Now Saun looked frightened as well as worried. "We don't know what to do," she said.

"Well, don't worry," Pearl said. "We'll help you, won't we, Dad?"

"Of course we will. Do you have an address there?"

Saun handed him the paper, and he studied it. "The address is Cotton Tree Drive. Let's go ask someone where that is. Someone with a map."

Saun and Ping seemed very glad to have help.

They all went back to the information booth, where a man with a big smile looked at a map for them. When he showed them where Cotton Tree Drive was, Mr. Kerrigan said, "Look at that. That's only a few blocks from where we'll be staying. You kids can go along with us."

"Oh, that would be wonderful!" Saun said. A look of relief washed over her face, and Ping said, "Thank you very much, sir."

Seth took Ping's hand. "You just stay with us. You'll be all right."

Pearl went to Saun, and the two girls also held hands as they left the terminal.

Outside, they got on the double-decker bus that was waiting.

"I'm surprised that nearly everyone speaks English here," Duffy said.

"Well, Hong Kong's been an international city for a long time. You could probably get along without speaking Chinese at all."

The bus took them on a forty-minute trip. It crossed over two bridges—Mr. Kerrigan said they were on the longest suspension bridge in the world for trains and cars—and went through the Western Tunnel to Hong Kong Island.

Juan, perhaps feeling he wasn't getting enough

attention, began to tell a story about a bridge that had collapsed. His brother and sisters knew Juan well enough to ignore him, but Saun and Ping did not. When he said, "And so the bridge collapsed, and everybody fell in the water," Duffy saw that Ping was very frightened.

She thumped Juan on the arm. "Stop that! You're scaring Ping and Saun."

Instantly, of course, Juan tapped her back, and their father reached out and pulled him away. "Enough of that, or I'll separate you two," he said.

Duffy turned to Saun and Ping, saying, "Don't pay any attention to Juan. He's just a show-off."

"I am not a show-off!"

"Yes, you are," Duffy said. "You're always trying to be the center of attention."

"Not either." He turned to the Chinese woman sitting beside him and said, *"Nay ho ma?"*

The woman looked surprised, then rattled off a long sentence in Chinese.

"What did you say, and what did she say?" Seth demanded.

"Nay ho ma means 'Hello, how are you?' I learned that."

"So what did she say?"

"I don't know. I haven't gotten that far yet."

Saun smiled. "She said she's very well thank you and hopes that you have a good day."

"I understood that!" Pearl said. "I wasn't sure I would remember any Chinese."

Perhaps Juan was jealous because Pearl could speak a language he could not. But it seemed he had learned a couple more Chinese words. He started saying, *"Aye yah! Aye yah!"* over and over again.

"What does *aye yah* mean?" Mr. Kerrigan asked, looking bewildered.

Pearl grinned. "It sort of means 'good grief.'"

When they came to the end of the tunnel, Mr. Kerrigan told them, "The hotel we'll stay in is going to be a nice one. I think you'll like it."

"Will we get to sightsee any?"

"Oh, sure. The hotel is right across from the Botanical and Zoological Gardens."

"You mean a zoo?"

"A small one, I think, and lots of flowers."

He went on telling them about what they would see. "And all of this is, more or less, right in the middle of Hong Kong Island."

"Has the hotel got a swimming pool?" Juan asked.

"According to the brochure, it has. And it's got a badminton court."

"That's good." Juan turned to Saun and said, "Do you play badminton?"

"A little."

"Good. I'll give you some lessons. I can beat all these guys."

This was true enough, but it sounded boastful to Duffy.

Saun said, "I would be very grateful if you give me some badminton lessons."

"I'm looking forward to visiting some of the churches here in Hong Kong," Mr. Kerrigan said. "We want to find a good one, and we don't have long."

"We'll find one, Dad," Pearl said. "We always find a good church."

After a while Duffy leaned over and whispered to Pearl, "We're being a little bit like the Good Samaritan, aren't we?"

"What do you mean?"

"I mean we saw the Li kids, and they needed help, and we helped them. I think that's what the Lord wanted us to do. That's what the story of the Good Samaritan is all about."

"We didn't do much."

But Duffy shook her head. "A little means a lot when you're lonely and afraid."

Pearl suddenly smiled. "I remember when I first came to live with you. How much time you spent trying to cheer me up. I don't know what I would have done if it hadn't been for you, Duffy."

Duffy reached over and hugged Pearl. "That's what sisters are for," she whispered.

TOO MANY PEOPLE

The double-decker bus rolled onto Hong Kong Island, and as soon as it stopped the Kerrigans got out. It took some doing to find their luggage, for others were doing the same thing. As a matter of fact, people were bumping into each other. It was harder on the youngsters because most of the passengers were grownups.

"I wish I was seven feet tall," Juan grumbled. "Then we'd see who'd go first."

"You're always wanting to be something you're not, Juan," Seth said. "Why don't you just settle for what you are?"

"You know what the pastor said," Pearl added. "If you look in a mirror and would change anything, you're not happy with the way God made you, and that's wrong."

Juan could not argue with this. He himself had heard the pastor say so. "Well"—he shrugged —"I'm happy enough with how good-looking I am. I'd just like to be a little taller—but there's still time for that."

"I doubt if you'll ever be seven feet tall," Seth said. "And why would you want to be? Think how hard it would be to get a bed long enough to sleep on."

They got onto another bus then—the one that would take them to their hotel. As it made its way through the streets, Duffy stared out with amazement. Everywhere she looked she saw bicycles. It seemed that there were hundreds—maybe even thousands.

Suddenly Juan pointed. "Look, there's a buggy being pulled by a *man!*"

Everyone looked in the direction in which Juan was pointing. Duffy saw a small carriage being pulled, indeed, by a man.

"That's a rickshaw," Pearl said. "I remember them."

"Why don't they just put a motor on it instead of having some guy pull it?"

"Oh, rickshaws are just for tourists today," Duffy said. "I read that in the book we got about Hong Kong."

"That's right," their dad said. "Years ago, before there were such things as automobiles, rickshaws were the taxis of the East. Instead of horses, men who could get no other work pulled them. They called the men *coolies.*"

As they wound on down the packed street, Duffy was also stunned at the lack of parking space for cars. There seemed to be none. The traffic went right up to the sidewalks, and these were cluttered with stands occupied by peddlers selling everything imaginable.

Juan spotted another rickshaw and then boasted, "I bet I could pull one of those."

"I wish we had one at home." Duffy winked at Pearl. "Then I wouldn't have to walk anywhere. You could just pull me to school or to town or when we go swimming. Why don't we get one of those? I'm sure you'd like it, Juan."

Juan knew when he was being teased. He said, "I'm not about to pull you anywhere, Duffy. You can walk."

"You probably couldn't pull it anyway," Seth said. "It takes a real strong person to pull that thing. Especially when it's loaded with two people." He pointed to one rickshaw that was going by. Two very large and overweight Americans were in it, and the young man who was pulling it was huffing and puffing.

"Oh, I could pull that! It wouldn't be any trouble for me."

"You couldn't, either!" Duffy said, and an argument broke out at once.

Mr. Kerrigan placed one hand on Duffy's neck

and the other on Juan's. He squeezed and pulled their heads closer. "Now look here, you two. I'm not going to listen to you fuss and quarrel all the time we're in Hong Kong. You can think what you please, but outwardly you've got to show more manners for each other."

"Sure, Dad," Juan said quickly. "You hear what he said, Duffy?"

"Did *I* hear what he said? You're the one that's always starting these things."

"And there you go again." Mr. Kerrigan sighed. He released them and then patted each on the shoulder. "Please try to show a little self-restraint, will you?"

The bus threaded its way along the crowded streets. At one point Mr. Kerrigan said, "Have you noticed how the past and the present kind of melt together here?" He pointed. "Look at those wooden boats bobbing up and down there."

"They're right next to those huge ocean liners," Seth said. "I wonder if they're for tourists just like the rickshaws."

"I don't think so," Pearl said. "I think people live on them."

"Live on those little boats!"

"Oh yes! In China, there are boat cities everywhere along the sea. Some babies are born on boats and spend their whole lives on them."

"Hey, that wouldn't be bad," Juan said. "You could go fishing anytime you wanted to."

"You'd get tired of that," Seth put in.

Duffy was looking out at something else. "See those old crumbling buildings right next to a new skyscraper."

"That's the past and the present bumping heads," her dad said. "And look at that. There's a Rolls Royce."

"What's a Rolls Royce?" Pearl asked.

"One of the most expensive automobiles they make," Juan said importantly. He always liked to dispense information. "And it's right alongside a rickshaw. "

"I'd rather have the Rolls Royce, I think." Duffy grinned.

"So would I."

The bus crawled. It could go no faster than those riding bicycles and often went slower.

Once, when they came to a full stop, Mr. Kerrigan said, "What are they selling over there? That vendor across the street? The sign's in Chinese."

Pearl looked. "He's selling chicken feet."

"What does anybody want with chicken feet?" Seth asked.

"To make chicken feet soup, I suppose."

"Chicken feet soup. That's as bad as that bird's nest soup," Duffy said. She gave a shudder. "I wouldn't want to eat either one."

"Do the Chinese people *really* eat bird's nest soup, Pearl?" Seth asked curiously.

Saun, who had been just listening to all of

31

this, interrupted. "Oh yes. Our mother would fix bird's nest soup for us even in Los Angeles."

"A real bird's nest?" Juan asked. "It doesn't sound like that would taste like anything."

"It's a special kind of nest," Saun explained. "The birds glue the little twigs together with some kind of special stuff. It's the special stuff that makes it good to eat."

"I bet it would be crunchy," Juan said, "but I think I'd rather have a nice, juicy steak."

"Look at that place. They're selling octopus," Seth said, pointing at another vendor. His sign was written in both Chinese and English. "Who'd want to eat an old octopus?"

"Nearly all Asian people on the coast like to eat octopus," Ping said. He turned to Seth. "Maybe you can come and eat dinner with us and try some squid."

"OK," Seth said. "I'll try almost anything once, even squid—or bird's nest soup."

"And look at that," Juan said, pointing. "Those guys are riding bicycles and talking on cell phones at the same time. I always thought they used cell phones just in America."

"As a matter of fact, Juan," his father said, "there's a pretty good chance that most of the cell phones in the States were made right here in Hong Kong or some other part of Asia."

The bus trip was slow, but the Kerrigan kids did not mind. It was interesting. The Li children did not say much, though, and Duffy knew that they were worried. Once she squeezed Saun's hand. "I bet your grandparents are very nice. You're going to have a good time living with them."

"I hope so. We can't even remember them very well," Saun said.

"They're sure to be nice people, and you're going to have a good life over here. It's lucky you can speak some Chinese."

"It was a little hard to keep it up, but our parents made us speak it at home. They always thought we might come back to Hong Kong someday. I guess it's a good thing they made us learn."

"Hey, what's that place over there?" Juan asked, looking out the window.

"Oh, that must be Hong Kong Park," Saun said. "It's very big. Our parents used to tell us about it."

Then they passed a large building that had a sign on it saying "Flagstaff House Museum of Tea Ware."

"A museum of tea cups!" Pearl cried. "I'd like to go in there. Can we go, Dad?"

"Yeah," Duffy said. "I'd like to see that, too."

"Sure. We can take that in," he agreed.

"Aw, who wants to see a bunch of old teacups? We can see cups any time," said Juan.

"The Chinese are experts at making fine plates, cups, and saucers. That's why good dishes are called 'china,'" Mr. Kerrigan said. "If you went to

Pennsylvania, you'd want to see how they make steel. Well, when you're in Hong Kong you'll want to see their china, so we'll spend some time taking that in."

Juan muttered, "Aw, that's for girls."

"Not at all. Some of the biggest teacup collectors in the world are men. And a lot of the people who make the teacups are men." Then Mr. Kerrigan said, "You'll have your chance, fellas, to see whatever appeals to guys. We've got to let the girls see their teacups. I'd like to see them myself."

The bus turned down Cotton Tree Drive, and the Li children both looked up at Mr. Kerrigan. "I think this is the street our grandparents live on," Saun Li said.

"Yes, this is it," he said. He looked for house numbers. "We'll just go with you to be sure that you get there all right."

This involved some doing, for the Kerrigans had to get off the bus with all their luggage. When they did, Mr. Kerrigan said, "I'll stay here and watch all the luggage. Duffy, why don't you and Seth go to the door with Saun and Ping to be sure they're in the right place and that their grandparents are home."

"OK, Dad," Duffy said. "Come on, Saun. Come on, Ping." She thought the Li children looked very relieved.

The Lis had only one suitcase apiece, but they had to struggle with them.

"Hey, we'll carry those," Juan said.

"Yes, we'll carry those," Seth said, taking Ping's suitcase from him. "We'll all go—except for you, Dad."

"I'll be right here. There's the place, right over there."

There was not a chance of getting lost, for the house they were looking for was only three doors down. "I guess this is it," Saun said.

"Ring the bell."

Saun Li did, rather timidly. No one came for a long time.

"Maybe they're not home," Duffy said.

But even as she spoke, the door opened just a crack, and then an older Chinese woman opened it. She took one look at the Li children and gave a glad cry. She said something in Chinese and hurried forward to embrace them both.

"Well, I guess we've done our duty," Juan said.

Saun said, "This is my grandmother. She doesn't speak much English, but she wants to thank you for bringing us."

"Tell her it was our pleasure," Duffy said.

But Pearl, speaking rather haltingly, said a sentence in Chinese.

Mrs. Li's face broke into a smile. She bowed several times and spoke rapidly.

"What did she say, Pearl?"

"I think she said we must come back and visit

and have a meal with them while we're in Hong Kong."

"Tell her we'd like to."

After saying good-bye, they walked back to where their father stood waiting and watching.

"Everything all right?" he asked.

"Oh yes. We met their grandmother," Duffy said. "She wants us to come back and have a meal with them."

"That could be a good place for me to get some fine pictures—if you don't think they'd mind."

"Mrs. Li seemed very nice," Pearl said. "Eating with them would be fun. Then we could visit with Saun and Ping. I'll bet they'll be lonesome for a while."

"Well, did you think to get the phone number?"

"Saun got it for us," Duffy said. She handed the slip of paper to her father, who folded it and put it into his wallet.

"Well, let's get back on a bus."

They had to wait for a time, but finally another bus came along. It was a matter of loading all their baggage on again. They found seats while the bus continued, and before long it was stopping in front of a huge building across from a beautiful hillside garden. There were flowers of all kinds and all colors, so bright they almost hurt Duffy's eyes.

"Here's our hotel, kids."

"Wow, look at that!" Duffy said, still staring at the hillside. "Let's go explore the garden."

"No, we've got to get settled and get the bags put away first."

Juan said, "Dad, we've got to get something to eat. I'm starving!"

"As soon as we get registered, we will."

Juan staggered and held his stomach. Then he clutched his head. "I'm going to faint," he moaned. "Are you trying to abuse me, Dad?"

"I might if you don't quit showing off," his father teased. "Now, come on. You're no hungrier than the rest of us."

They made their way inside the hotel and checked in. The clerk, a small, young Chinese with warm, brown eyes was very friendly. He put them in adjoining rooms on the third floor. Mr. Kerrigan said he wanted three rooms this time so he could have quiet to do his work.

They rode the elevator, which the clerk had called a "lift" just as they did in England. Duffy, especially, was anxious to see what the rooms looked like.

"We'll check ours first," Juan said. "If we don't like it, we'll take yours, Duffy. You girls don't care where you sleep anyway."

"You will not!" she said.

Mr. Kerrigan handed Juan his key. Juan opened the door, and they crowded inside.

"It's so little!" Juan said, sounding disappointed.

"Remember, the Chinese people are smaller than we are," Mr. Kerrigan said. "But it *is* a little bit tiny."

The room had no windows. It did have a small balcony, barely large enough for two people to stand on. The furniture was mostly made of shiny black, lacquered wood. There were many baskets, small tables, and all sorts of wood carvings. Chinese landscape murals hung on the walls, and they discovered that lush green plants were hanging on the small balcony.

Juan and Duffy went out onto the balcony, and the others looked out from behind them.

"Why does it look more crowded here than it does back home?" Juan asked.

"I know why," Duffy said. "I've been reading about it. Hong Kong is only a small place, but there are fourteen thousand people for every square mile."

"How many people per square mile are there in America, Duffy?" her dad asked, smiling. "Remember?"

"Only seventy-five."

"Yep, that's true. Hong Kong is one of the most densely populated places in the world."

Juan suddenly appeared to be falling off the balcony.

"Grab him!" Mr. Kerrigan cried in alarm.

Seth and Duffy caught Juan and pulled him back.

"What's the matter with you?" Seth cried.

"I'm fainting from lack of food."

"Oh, come on, then." His father grinned. "Let's get our luggage settled, and then we'll go out and eat."

"About time," Juan said. He made a face at Duffy. "Just stick with me, Duffy. I'll order your supper for you."

"I'll order my own supper, thank you," Duffy sniffed and turned around. "Come on, Pearl. Let's go see our room."

A MEAL
TO REMEMBER

As soon as the Kerrigans left their hotel, Juan began eagerly searching for a place to eat. He begged to go into the first restaurant they saw. "Look, there's one that sells dim sum." He pointed to a sign. "Let's go in. I could eat a lot of dim sum."

"Dim sum isn't something you eat." Pearl giggled.

"What is it, then?" Juan demanded. "This is an eating place. Why are they advertising it?"

"Dim sum means a little snack."

"Oh. Well, that's not what I want. I want a big snack."

"I can't see how anybody can ever read Chinese writing," Duffy said. "It looks impossible."

"Chinese characters are interesting," Pearl said. "But I don't know many. Those characters there mean 'to touch the heart.'"

"Well, I don't need my heart touched," Juan said. "I need my stomach touched. Let's hurry up."

The Kerrigans managed to restrain Juan until they found a large restaurant. It was very crowded, and they had to wait in line, but finally they got seats.

A waiter came, who bowed several times and said in English, "What can I serve you, please, sirs?"

"Some of everything you've got," Juan said importantly.

"Now wait a minute, Juan. You don't want to do that. All Chinese restaurants have more food than even you could possibly eat."

"Well, all right. But I've warned you. I'm going to go into a feeding frenzy," Juan said.

Trolley after trolley of food was wheeled by them, and they got to choose food out of bamboo baskets. There were finely chopped meats, seafood, and vegetables wrapped in thin dough. On another cart were foods that were steamed, fried, and boiled.

Juan usually could not make up his mind, so he managed to take two of each.

Mr. Kerrigan warned him. "Slow down, son. There's more to eat where that came from."

"Well, it's not my fault. You shouldn't have made us wait so long."

"What's this?" he asked a waiter.

"That is steamed dumplings."

"I'll have some. And what's this?"

"Meatballs."

"I'll have half a dozen of those. And what's this?"

"Fried spring rolls."

"Sounds good. I'll try that. And what about this. Is it spareribs?"

"Yes sir."

"I'll have that."

The two girls stared at him. Even some of the people who were eating at adjoining tables stared.

"Juan, slow down. You've been brought up better than this. I'm ashamed of you."

"Sorry, Dad. I guess I just got carried away."

Once Duffy reached out to try a piece of fried spring roll from Juan's plate. He put his arms around the plate as if she were going to take it away from him.

Duffy laughed, but she said, "Juan, don't be so selfish. Share what you have."

"All right." Juan broke off a very small portion and dropped it onto her plate. "There. That ought to be enough."

"I hate to think about the stomachache you're going to have," Seth said.

After a while they started talking about their favorite part of the meal.

"I think this is my favorite dish," Juan decided. "What is it again, Pearl?"

"That's deep fried spring rolls filled with shredded pork."

"Well, it sure is good, but it's got other stuff in it, too."

"It's got chicken and mushrooms and bamboo shoots and bean sprouts," she said.

Juan laughed. "Just what I need. All the main food groups in one bite."

Finally even Juan was finished. They paid their bill, left a tip, and walked outside into the bright sunshine. A hubbub of people were coming and going in all directions.

As the Kerrigans walked down the busy street, looking in the stores, Duffy could see small altars for worship in nearly every shop. That seemed strange. They passed vendors selling bright orange octopus legs. Then they came to a dress shop that had a beautiful, long red dress in the window.

"That's a nice party dress," Duffy said.

"That's a wedding dress," Pearl told her.

Duffy grew more interested right away. "You mean brides wear *red* dresses? All brides?"

"Yes." Pearl smiled at Duffy's expression. "In America they wear white. I think red is a much prettier color."

"Well, a bride would sure be noticed if she wore that."

"What's that moving thing, Dad?" Seth asked suddenly.

Mr. Kerrigan looked and smiled. "Come on, and I'll show you."

They followed him to something that seemed

like an escalator, except that it didn't go up. It just went straight.

"It goes right into that building," Juan said.

"Get on," Mr. Kerrigan said. "We might as well rest our feet a while."

It turned out to be a moving sidewalk. It took them right into the store and down through the middle of it!

"Hey, this is a cool idea!" Juan said. "We can just go shopping without walking our legs off."

"It saves a little space, too," Mr. Kerrigan said. "As you've noticed, it's pretty crowded here in Hong Kong."

They had a great time traveling on the moving sidewalk, and, since the store was air-conditioned, it was nice to get cooled off from the heat outside.

Finally they got off the moving walkway and went down to the lower level of the store. Mr. Kerrigan had given each of them spending money to buy souvenirs and small gifts for their friends back home. But he warned them not to spend it all the first day, so Duffy was trying to be careful.

"I'm getting a little tired, Dad. I think I've got jet lag," she said.

"We all need to get a good night's rest."

"Dad, on the way back could we go by and see how Saun and Ping are doing?" Seth asked.

"Maybe we can try tomorrow, if we can find the house again."

"I would sure like to see Ping again," Seth said. "It seems like he needs a friend."

"Saun needs a friend, too," Pearl said. "I could tell she was lonesome."

"Seems you four are always finding kids that are lonely. Remember Joe Purvis back in Australia?"

"Well, he *was* lonely. He was living out in the big middle of nowhere," Juan said. He looked at the busy crowd around him. "Ping and Saun sure aren't going to lack for company here."

But Duffy knew better. "You can be lonely in a big crowd. It's better to have one real friend than have hundreds of people around that you don't know very well."

"You're right, honey, and we'll sure go back and see how Saun and Ping are doing," their dad said. "Now let's go try to get over this jet lag."

5

TWO
SAD KIDS

"It's time to get up." Pearl was shaking Duffy and pulling off her covers.

"Go away."

But her sister ignored Duffy's protests. When Duffy tried to burrow under the pillow, Pearl simply pulled it away. "Get up, you sleepyhead! You're going to sleep your life away."

Duffy blinked and ruffled her hair. "What time is it?" she muttered, sitting up.

"Seven o'clock. The day's half gone."

"Seven o'clock! What are you talking about? We don't have to go anywhere today."

"Yes, we do. We're going out with Dad to take pictures. Remember? Now get out of bed."

But Duffy threw herself back down. Pulling up

the covers again, she grumbled, "I don't have to get up yet." She turned over, face down.

All was quiet for a while. Then suddenly a small stream of water dribbled onto Duffy's neck.

"*Yeow!* What are you doing?" Coming off the bed, Duffy looked wildly around. Then she saw Pearl's grin and the glass of water in her hand, and she frowned. "You trying to drown me?"

"I don't think a few drops of water will drown you. Now come on, Duffy. Get ready to go."

"I suppose I might as well. I'm wide awake now."

The two girls dressed. Pearl put on a blue denim skirt and a short-sleeved white blouse decorated with tiny pink bows on the collar.

Duffy looked at her sister's outfit and shook her head. She never could understand why anyone would wear something with pink on it. She searched through her suitcase until she found a pair of white shorts and her favorite lime green T-shirt. Sighing with satisfaction she put these on, then put on a pair of lime green socks and her new Keds.

They brushed their hair, and by the time they were finished a loud knock sounded on the door.

"That must be Juan," Pearl said. "He always sounds like he's trying to break the door down. Come in, Juan," she yelled.

"I can't. It's locked."

"Oh, I forgot!" Pearl ran over and opened the door.

Juan was wearing one of his more colorful outfits, which was saying a lot. He had on a pair of dark purple shorts that were a little big and hung down below his knees. His silky shirt had bright purple, yellow, orange, and green stripes. He had pulled his tube socks up so high that they came to where his shorts ended.

"Well, you won't get lost in Hong Kong in that outfit. If you do, we'll put a notice in the paper—'Lost. One boy looking like a rainbow.'"

"You like it, don't you?" Juan said, walking around for them to admire his clothes. "I knew you would."

"Very colorful," Duffy said. "Where's Seth?"

"He's with Dad. We're all ready to go eat. I'm starved."

"You're always starved." Duffy said.

The three met their father and Seth in the lobby, and at once Seth said, "I bet you're hungry, aren't you, Juan?"

"How'd you guess?" Juan grinned. "Let's go somewhere and get bacon and eggs and pancakes and grits and biscuits."

"That's an American breakfast. We'd have to find an American cafe for that," Mr. Kerrigan told him. "We'll just take what comes."

They found a very nice restaurant, but they did not get exactly the breakfast that Juan had longed for. Instead they ordered from the typical Chinese breakfast menu. On the menu were "*bing*" (pancakes), "*tang*" (a soybean milk soup), "*gao*" (doughnuts), "*bao*" (buns), "*zhou*" (rice porridge), and "*mian*" (noodles), all served with soup or milk for the drink of the morning.

Duffy and Pearl were not very hungry, so they each had a bun and the porridge. Seth and their dad had pancakes and soup. And Juan ordered it all. As he was finishing off his plate, he talked about all he wanted to do while they were in Hong Kong.

Mr. Kerrigan listened, but then he said, "We couldn't do all that if we stayed here a year, Juan."

"Well, let's do all we can. So come on, you all. Stop fooling around. We've got to get going."

"Fooling around!" Seth said, lifting his eyebrows. "I like that! We've been waiting for half an hour for you to finish eating, and now *we're* fooling around."

When they left the restaurant, Seth insisted on carrying his dad's large camera case. It was stuffed with different cameras and film. He asked as they walked along, "What are you going to photograph today, Dad?"

"Not quite sure. We're going to start with Hong Kong Park. Maybe we'll see something of interest there."

At the park they simply walked around for a while. Mr. Kerrigan did take pictures of a few individuals, but finally he said, frowning, "What I need is something a little bit more . . . special."

"What's going on over there?" Juan asked. "It looks like some kind of a game." And he was off like a shot.

The others had no choice but to follow him. They all arrived at an open spot where about twenty men dressed in white were doing some sort of exercise.

"This must be some kind of martial arts, I would guess," Mr. Kerrigan said.

A Chinese gentleman who was also watching turned and said in perfect English, "It is. You are a visitor here?" He was a tall, older man.

"Yes, we are."

"Then we welcome you to Hong Kong." The man smiled. "Would you like to know what this is?"

"Very much," Mr. Kerrigan said. He got out his favorite camera and began to photograph the men, who were doing a difficult and unusual exercise.

"This is called tai chi chuan. It is a highly disciplined physical routine. It involves more than two hundred individual movements."

"Is it a martial art?"

"It is closely connected. The idea is to exercise every muscle of one's body and to bring peace and balance to one's self."

"You know, sir, I never really understood

that," Mr. Kerrigan said. "I think, of course, that one should have health of the body and health of the soul, but I fail to see how making the body healthy could make the soul well."

The Chinese gentleman just looked at him and then shrugged. "It must be difficult for an American to understand."

Duffy and Pearl stood together, watching the exercising men. They moved slowly at times, very gracefully, and then they would whip around almost with the speed of light, it seemed.

"It looks a little bit like ballet," Duffy decided. "But sort of in a masculine way."

Juan didn't think that at all. "It doesn't look anything like ballet. You know what I always thought about ballet? I just wondered why they didn't get taller girls so they didn't have to walk around on their toes all the time."

"You are uncouth and have no culture!" Seth told him.

"I'm as couth as you are, and I've got as much culture as you have. I can do what they're doing, anyway. Just watch."

Juan began stepping around, trying to imitate the actions of the athletes. Most of the people watching looked amused. Laughter went up as Juan jumped sideways, twisted his feet—and then fell flat on his back.

"I did that on purpose," he said, quickly scrambling up.

"Oh, sure you did!" Duffy said sarcastically. "Do it again and show us how graceful you can fall down."

Juan glared at her and then went back to his shadowboxing.

Mr. Kerrigan moved here and there, getting as many pictures as he could. Duffy could never understand why he took so many. The camera was clicking almost constantly. But he had told them many times, "You have to take a hundred pictures to get one very good one." And that day he must have taken more than a hundred. He was very quick and managed to stay out of the way of the athletes while at the same time getting his shots.

Then he started interviewing one of the men and taking down on his tape recorder what the man said. Later, Duffy knew, he would write it all down.

Juan and Seth too began talking to some of the other athletes who had finished exercising.

Suddenly Pearl said, "Look over there. There's Saun and Ping!"

"My, they look unhappy," Duffy said.

"They sure do. Let's go see what's the matter."

The two girls ran over to their new friends and greeted them. "Hi, Ping. Hi, Saun."

"Oh, hello," Saun said. "What are you doing here?"

"Dad wanted to take some pictures, and now

he's interviewing some of those fellows who did the shadowboxing."

The girls talked with Saun and Ping for a while, and it was very obvious that they were not happy.

"What's the matter, Saun?" Pearl said at last. "Is something wrong?"

Saun looked at Ping, and tears came into her eyes.

"Don't cry. It'll be all right. Tell us about it."

"Well, we just don't like it over here," Saun said.

"Your grandparents aren't mean to you, are they?"

"Oh no, nothing like that!" Saun said, acting a little shocked. "But they don't speak much English, and they don't really like anything American."

"Oh, that's too bad."

"They didn't want our parents to go to America in the first place, and they're still upset about it. We want to go back to the States!"

Just then Seth and Juan came over. Seth put his arm around Ping's shoulder and said, "Hey, buddy! It's good to see you again."

Ping brightened up a little, but when Seth asked if something was wrong, he too said, "We just don't like it here, Seth."

"Well, we'll have to do something about that. Hang in here for just a minute."

* * *

Seth ran back to his father, who was putting away his camera. "Hey, Dad, Saun and Ping are over here. They're real unhappy."

"What's wrong with them?"

"They say they don't like living here in Hong Kong. They want to go back to the States—and they can't. Could we help somehow? What do you say we go by and see their grandparents? Maybe make friends with them."

"That sounds like a good idea, Seth. We could do that. Let's ask the kids if their grandparents are home."

Mr. Kerrigan stuffed his camera in the bag, and they joined the rest of the children. "Hi, Ping. Hello, Saun."

"Hello, Mr. Kerrigan," they both said at once.

"I'd like to meet your grandparents and maybe see where you live. You think that would be all right?"

"I don't know," Saun said. "They don't speak much English."

"Well, you do. You can be our interpreter. How about we have some lunch and then go back to your place?"

Saun looked a little apprehensive, but she exchanged glances with Ping, who nodded. "I would like that. You will have to remember that they are old, and they don't know any place except Hong Kong. They're very old-fashioned."

"Well, I'd like very much to get to know them. We all would," Mr. Kerrigan said.

"Great. Let's go," Juan said.

Mr. Kerrigan, with Duffy at his side, started in the direction of Cotton Tree Drive. Pearl walked along with Saun, holding her hand, and Seth stuck close to Ping, talking and keeping a hand on his shoulder.

"I feel so sorry for those two, Dad," Duffy murmured.

"It must be pretty tough on them being thrown into a whole different world. Well, maybe we can find a way to help a little."

"We've got to do all we can for them while we're here."

"You're a good girl, Duffy Kerrigan."

Duffy smiled up at him and took his hand. "And you're a good dad, James Kerrigan."

MR. AND MRS. LI

The Kerrigans and the Li children approached Grandmother and Grandfather Li's small house. Ping walked to the large red door, reached up, and rang the bell.

"Why do you have to ring the bell to your own house, Ping?" Seth asked.

"We don't have a key, but our grandparents are nearly always here. They let us in."

"They don't go out much then?" Mr. Kerrigan asked.

"No. Hardly ever. All they do is stay at home. Most of the things they need they have delivered."

The door opened then, and the little woman peered out through the crack again. She looked rather startled at seeing the Americans on her step. And then she saw her grandchildren. She opened the door and said something quickly in Chinese.

Saun said, "Oh no, Grandmother, nothing is wrong." Then she repeated the same thing in Chinese. She explained, speaking slowly in English, "These are the kind friends from the airplane, remember? The ones who helped Ping and me so much."

Mrs. Li's eyes brightened at that, and she stepped back. She said in heavily accented English, "Hello. Please will you to come in."

The Kerrigans stepped inside, and—as at the hotel—Duffy was shocked at how small the room was. The house was beautiful, though, and Duffy said so. "What a nice home you have, Mrs. Li."

Mrs. Li apparently understood this, for she said, "Thank you ver' much."

Indeed the room was beautiful. There were murals on the walls and silk screens with Chinese garden designs. These screens separated the rooms in the little house. As a matter of fact, Saun told them, instead of having walls, the Chinese people often just put up screens. That way one large room could serve as the living room and dining room and kitchen.

"These are beautiful wood carvings," Mr. Kerrigan said, moving closer to look at one.

"My husband, he is good woodcarver."

"Your husband did these?" Duffy said. "That's wonderful! I wish I could do something like that."

Mrs. Li bowed low and said, "Thank you. Ver' good."

The small room had many carvings and brilliantly colored vases. Some of them had gold designs. Black lacquer tables were here and there, and Duffy and her family walked around admiring the art of it all.

"I think the Chinese people are more artistic than Americans," Mr. Kerrigan said.

This idea was somewhat difficult to understand, so Saun had to tell her grandmother in Chinese. Mrs. Li said something rapidly, and Saun said, "She thanks you very much for your kind remarks—and she would like to know if you would like to have some tea."

"That would be very good, wouldn't it, kids?"

All the Kerrigans bowed, as they had seen Mrs. Li and many others in Hong Kong do. Duffy decided that bowing was very common here. It was almost like nodding your head in America.

When Mrs. Li left the room, Saun and Ping showed the visitors some art that they had missed. But soon Mrs. Li came back in with her husband. Mr. Li was a head taller than his wife, though still considerably shorter than Mr. Kerrigan.

"This my husband. He speak bad English."

"I'm sure his English is better than my Chinese," Mr. Kerrigan said with a smile.

Mr. Li must have understood this, for he smiled, too, and said, "We honored to be your guest."

If Saun wanted to correct her grandfather's English, apparently she decided not to.

Mr. Li suddenly put out his hand, and Mr. Kerrigan shook it. "Welcome to home," Grandfather Li said.

Mrs. Li busied herself with fixing tea. Saun went to help her, and soon they were all sitting on the floor around a very low table. The tea was excellent, and there were small sweet cakes to go with it. Juan put a whole one into his mouth, and Duffy reached over and slapped his hand when he reached for another. "Don't be such a pig!"

Mr. and Mrs. Li seemed to think this was very funny. They understood that much of what she had said.

"Well, he *is* a pig, Mrs. Li."

"I am not! I just know good cooking when I see it and when I taste it."

Trying to have a conversation was somewhat difficult, but the Lis relaxed a bit as time went on.

After a while Mr. Kerrigan said, "I am a photographer. Would it be permissible to take some pictures of your home sometime?"

This took some explanation from Saun in Chinese, and the Lis seemed somewhat frightened by the idea.

"Perhaps this is not good manners. If so, you'll have to excuse me," Mr. Kerrigan said.

"It's all right. They just don't understand new

things," Saun said. "Even things like cameras and what you do."

"Mrs. Li, perhaps we could work out a trade," Duffy suggested.

"A trade?" Mrs. Li said. "What is trade?"

"You could let my dad take some pictures of you and your husband and your house. Then we could do something nice for you."

"What you do?"

"Oh . . . something you like."

Mr. Li had been trying to follow this, and when Saun explained the conversation, he said rather painfully, "Yiss. You do something."

"What can we do, Mr. Li?" Duffy said quickly.

"You be good with my grandchildren."

"Oh, be friends with your grandchildren?"

"Yiss."

"That's not hard to do. We'll come every day, and they can show us around Hong Kong, and you can come, too."

"No. Too old."

"Not at all," Mr. Kerrigan said. "I'd like it very much if you and your wife would go out and have dinner with us at a nice restaurant."

When this was finally explained to Mr. Li, he brightened and nodded. "Thank you. You ver' good."

And the arrangements were made.

When they finally left the house, Mr. Kerrigan said, "They're very nice people."

"They really are—but so old-fashioned. They don't even have a TV," Juan said. "That's what Ping told me."

"They don't have a TV? Why, most of the TV sets in the world are made in Hong Kong or Japan. I wonder why they don't have one."

"Maybe they can't afford one," Duffy said.

"Oh, I think they could. They had some very fine things in their house," Mr. Kerrigan said slowly. "Anyhow, it's something we may find out someday."

The Kerrigans began spending some time every day at the Li house. Both Mr. and Mrs. Li were eager to learn more English, and they insisted that Mr. Kerrigan and the children speak only English while they were there.

"That won't be hard," Seth said with a grin. "That's all we do speak."

Mr. Kerrigan often went picture taking by himself, and Juan insisted on going to the Hong Kong Park nearly every morning to watch the tai chi chuan practice. He said he was learning some of the exercises that they had mastered.

Even Mr. and Mrs. Li went out with the Kerrigans one day, and they seemed to enjoy themselves very much. They all made a trip to the Tea Ware Museum, and even the boys went through it. The Flagstaff House was the oldest colonial building in Hong Kong, and it was filled with very old pieces of china. They also saw how tea was made.

The girls ooh-ed and ah-ed over the beautiful pieces, but the boys quickly tired of this. They all went next to a dim sum restaurant. Mr. and Mrs. Li said they enjoyed the snacks very much.

One morning Duffy said to Saun, "You've made our visit here so nice, Saun. We love your family."

Saun was smiling. "And I don't know what we would have done if you hadn't come. My grandparents like your father a great deal. They see that Americans are very nice. They are much happier now."

"And Dad says he's been getting some great pictures. When he gets them developed, I'll bet he'll have some good ones of your grandparents."

"They really want pictures of Ping and me."

"Well, there'll be those too. Now let's go over to the park. We can watch Juan try to do tai chi chuan and fall flat on his face."

THE ZOO

What would you like to do, kids? Today you get to choose."

Mr. Kerrigan had taken the family out to breakfast, and as they sat there finishing up, he grinned at his small crew. "I've got a lot to do tomorrow, but today I've got some time to spare, so I thought I'd let you do anything you wanted."

"That sounds cool, Dad!" Juan said. "That's what I like. Just doing anything I want."

"I thought you might feel that way, Juan."

Then Juan gave his father an odd look. "Uh . . . Dad, you wouldn't punish me for something I didn't do, would you?"

"Of course not," Mr. Kerrigan said at once. "That wouldn't be fair."

"That's good. I didn't finish my math yet, so

now we're both agreed that I don't have to be punished for something I didn't do."

"You're not going to let him get away with that, are you, Dad?" Seth asked.

"I don't think so, but we'll take it up later. Now, what's on the agenda for today?"

"I'd like to go to the zoo," Seth said. "I always like zoos."

"I don't like them so much," Pearl said.

"Why not?" Seth inquired.

"Oh, animals were made to be free, and it just seems sad to coop them up."

"Well, in some ways that may be true," Duffy said. "But think of it like this—the animals have a pretty rough time out in the wild. Sometimes they can't get enough food, so they starve to death. And when they get sick, they just die. But when they're in a zoo, if they get sick they have a vet calling on them right away."

"That's right," Juan said, "and they get three square meals a day, I'll bet. Every day."

"I know," suggested Duffy. "Let's get Ping and Saun. I bet they'd like to come to the zoo with us."

"That's a fine idea, Duffy," agreed Mr. Kerrigan. "We'll do that."

"The Hong Kong zoo is a zoo *and* a kind of garden, isn't it, Dad?" Pearl asked.

"Sure is."

"Then maybe we can look at the flowers and the plants too."

"I don't like plants much except for Venus's-flytraps. I like to see them eat the flies," Juan said.

"You are gross, Juan," Duffy said. "Don't you ever have a normal thought?"

"Normal! I'm normal. I'm the most normal person I ever saw."

Everybody hooted at that, and then they left the restaurant.

Mr. Kerrigan had read up on the zoo. He told them, "There are about nine hundred birds in this zoo with about two hundred eighty different species."

Juan at once began telling an awful story about birds coming to peck out people's eyes and eating them.

Duffy reached over and pulled his hair. "Juan, stop telling those awful stories!"

"Well, birds have to eat, don't they?"

"Never mind that," their dad said. "Let's try to think of something pleasant for a change."

Juan could not go long without telling a joke. "Did you hear about the woman that went to the psychiatrist?"

"No, but I'm afraid we're going to," Seth said.

"Well, the psychiatrist said, 'What's your trouble?' and she said, 'I'm just fond of pancakes.' And the doctor said, 'Is that all? Why, I like pancakes myself.'"

Juan looked around at his audience. "The woman said, 'You do, doctor? Really? Well, you'll have to come over to my house. I've got trunks and trunks full of them.'"

Everyone groaned. But he kept on telling corny jokes all the way to the zoo.

The gardens were spread out on a hill called Victoria Peak. Flowers of one kind or another were always in bloom there, they learned, so the dark green hill was dotted with many different colors. They passed little signs naming the trees and plants, and Pearl found this very interesting. She was walking along slowly, holding Saun's hand and reading the signs. "Burmese rosewood tree. And this is an Indian rubber tree."

"And see here," Seth said. "This is a camphor tree."

"I never heard of a camphor tree," Duffy said.

"Camphor is used in medicines to help you breathe when you get sick," their father said.

"Oh, that's right. It was in a salve you used to use when we got stuffed-up noses. I remember that."

Juan soon tired of reading the names of trees, and he began shadowboxing, the way he had seen it done in Hong Kong Park.

"Look at me! I can do it!" he yelled. He tried one of the fancy movements, but actually he was not very agile. He kept stumbling over his feet, and Mr. Kerrigan took a picture of him just as he happened to fall on his back.

"I'll make you an eight-by-ten enlargement of that, Juan," his dad said.

And Duffy told him, "I still think you'd better practice ballet first."

"No way, José!" Juan said. "All I need is a little more practice."

They saw many beautiful flowers as well as many animals and birds, and the morning passed quickly. But what Duffy found she liked most was how much Saun and Ping enjoyed their day. It gave her pleasure just to see the two youngsters skip and run. Almost always, Saun was with Pearl, and Ping was with Seth. They just seemed to pair off naturally.

Duffy said to her father, "I'm glad that Pearl and Seth are so good to those kids. They really need all the encouragement they can get."

"They sure do. Moving to the other side of the world was a rough blow for them," Mr. Kerrigan said. He suddenly raised his camera and took a picture of Duffy.

"Oh, Dad, I had my mouth wide open!"

"I know it. I've been trying to get a picture of you with your mouth wide open."

"You wouldn't have any trouble getting a picture of Juan that way," she said, laughing. "He's always blabbing."

"Juan's a lively one."

"I get irritated with him sometimes, but he is so much fun."

They watched while Juan moved around, trying to go through the intricate drill that he had seen the athletes perform. "I just need a little more practice," he said.

At noon they took time out to have a quick snack. It was a kind of delicious meat encased in a toasty crust. Juan, as usual, ate more than anyone else did.

"You're going to weigh a thousand pounds if you keep on eating like that, Juan," Seth told him as they left the restaurant.

"No, I won't. I'll work it all off." He started to whirl around again, making wild gestures with his arms and kicking out with his feet. But suddenly he stopped and stood very still. A most peculiar look came onto his face. "I think I won't exercise any more."

Mr. Kerrigan grinned. "About to get sick, are you?"

"Not me. I never get sick."

That was not true. Juan did get sick on occasion. It was obvious that he was feeling sick now. It calmed him down for a while.

They went back to the zoo. Seth thought the jaguars and the leopards were very interesting.

"They have beautiful coats, don't they? Look at that tiger over there. Isn't he something?"

"That fellow could make a meal out of you in one bite," Mr. Kerrigan said. They watched the huge tiger yawn and then stare out through the bars with pale eyes like green fire. "I'm glad those bars are there," he added.

"You can't get at him as long as they are, can you, Dad?" Duffy said with a sly grin and then laughed at her father's expression.

They moved on into the monkey house. Duffy liked the gibbons best, for they could swing with such ease. Their arms were tremendously long, and they could hold on with their feet as well. "I wish I could swing through the trees like that," she said.

"You'd have to look like one of them to do that," Juan said. "Come to think of it, you do look a little bit like that one right there."

"Oh, be quiet, Juan! Can't you say anything nice?"

Juan stopped in front of one of the cages. Inside was a large monkey with reddish fur, and he was staring straight at Juan.

"Look at this one," Juan said. "Hey, fella, can you do this?" Juan swung his arms up and around in one of the maneuvers he was trying to learn.

The monkey watching him did exactly the same thing.

"Did you see that!" Juan cried. "He did what I did!" He looked delighted. "Now watch this. Try this." He jumped high and turned around as best he could in midair.

The monkey leaped into the air and turned

around, too. He was much more graceful than Juan.

People gathered at the cage to watch. Everything that Juan did, the monkey did. And soon everyone began applauding. Mr. Kerrigan said, "That's really amazing. I wonder if that's a trained monkey."

"Oh, he's just Juan's half-brother, Dad," Duffy said loudly. "Except he's better looking and a lot more graceful."

Juan was in the midst of one of his gyrations. He swatted Duffy on the shoulder.

Instantly the monkey in the cage slapped another monkey. But that monkey didn't like it, and in seconds they were rolling, pulling hair, and biting at each other.

"That's what you ought to do to Juan," Seth told Duffy.

"No, thanks. I don't believe I want to do that. Juan is monkey enough for the two of us."

They wandered for a time longer, and soon Mr. Kerrigan was taking a picture of a beautiful orchid, which was in full bloom. The kids stood around waiting and watching as he carefully set the shutter and tried framing the flower in a dozen different ways. Nobody said anything until finally he took the picture.

"You sure do take a long time to take one picture, Dad," Juan complained. "Why don't you just shoot it?"

"The best pictures are those that take a lot of time. I've seen some of the pictures you've taken, Juan—people with their heads cut off or overexposed or taken with the camera pointed up at the sky."

"I'm just a natural photographer," Juan said airily. "I don't fool with the details."

"And that's the reason your pictures aren't good like Dad's," Duffy told him.

"Of course," Mr. Kerrigan said, "Juan plays the guitar better than I can, so I guess we're even." He began to put his equipment very carefully into the soft leather carrying bag. Then he said, "How about we go back to your house, Ping? I'll bet your grandparents have something good to snack on."

"Yes, and they like to have you come," Ping said. "Let's go."

THE CHURCH

The day after the visit to the zoo, Duffy's dad told the family they were going to go through a Buddhist temple.

"Of course, we're Christians," he explained to Duffy and Seth and Juan and Pearl, "and we don't believe that Buddha has any power, but I think it might be good for us at least to look at what so many Asians worship."

"I'd like to go," Duffy said quickly. "And we can take Saun and Ping with us, can't we?"

"Oh, yes. I'm sure you want to spend all the time you can with them."

The Kerrigans stopped by for Saun and Ping, and their grandparents were happy, indeed, for their grandchildren to have another outing. "You come back, and we eat tonight," Mrs. Li said.

"That would be a lot of trouble for you, wouldn't it?"

"No trouble. You come." She nodded her head, and Mr. Li, smiling, also said, "Come."

The group left the Lis and took the double-decker bus until they got to Victoria Harbor.

"How do we get to the other side?" Seth asked, looking across the water.

"We go on that ferry. It goes over to the New Territories."

The ferry ride was a fun trip for all of them. Fooling around, Juan nearly fell overboard once, but Mr. Kerrigan grabbed him by the belt and yanked him back.

After the ferry docked, they rode another bus for a while and after that got on a small, wood-burning train that was packed with sightseers. Mr. Kerrigan watched for a good opportunity and took several pictures while on the train.

As they rode along, the Li children began talking about how much happier they were since their grandparents could speak a little more English.

"I think at first they felt embarrassed trying to talk with us in English," Saun said. "But they're doing so very well now."

"English must be hard for native Chinese speakers to learn," Mr. Kerrigan said.

"I'll bet not as hard as it is for English-speaking people to learn Chinese," Saun said.

"Why is that?" Duffy asked curiously.

"Because of the tones in Chinese."

"What does that mean?" Seth asked.

"It means a word can have more than one meaning—depending on the way you say it. Like, when you say 'dog,' you pretty much always say it the same way in English, but the Chinese word for dog is different."

"How can it be different? A dog's a dog," Juan said.

"No, Chinese is different." She pronounced a Chinese word and then said, "That means 'dog.' But if you change the way you say it"—and she demonstrated—"it doesn't mean 'dog' anymore. It means 'shut the door.' And if you change it a little bit more, it would mean 'big black cloud.'"

"Wow!" Duffy said. "You'd have to have a good ear."

"I think that people who don't have a good ear for music have a lot of trouble with Chinese," Mr. Kerrigan said. "I tried to learn a little of it, and the words all sounded just alike to me. I couldn't hear the difference."

All the Kerrigans were interested in learning to speak a little Chinese. Since Pearl could speak some, she and Saun and Ping offered to teach them a few words.

But Mr. Kerrigan said, "No. No matter how hard I try, it all sounds the same to me. I guess I'll just have to keep you three as interpreters."

The train huffed to a stop at a small station where all the passengers got off. Then everybody followed the signs to a series of red-and-white buildings and visited the Po Fook Ancestral Worship Hall.

It was very interesting, but Juan, who had never heard of ancestor worship, thought that part was rather strange.

"You mean they really worship their great-great-great-grandpa?" he said to Duffy.

"Yes, and don't talk so loud. You might hurt their feelings."

"Well, I can understand being polite to old people in your family, but *worshiping* some great-great-great-grandfather—that doesn't make sense to me."

"I don't understand it, either," Duffy said. "But we can be polite. You remember how badly I got mixed up when we were in Africa. I couldn't understand the ways of the Masai people."

"And you say you can't understand this, either."

"No, I can't, but I can be polite about it. And I want you to be, too. I wouldn't hurt Saun and Ping's feelings for all the world."

"You think they've ever been to church?" Juan wondered.

"I don't know, but maybe we could take them with us when we go tomorrow—if their grandparents will let them."

They came to the point in the worship hall where there was a little pond with special fish and turtles. From there they took two hundred steps —the brochure said—to a temple that housed three large gold Buddhas.

It was all very strange to Duffy. In fact, she was disturbed by the experience.

And then Pearl asked Saun and Ping, "Are you two Buddhists?"

"No, our parents gave up Buddhism when they left China," Saun said.

"Are you anything?"

"We went to church in America a few times, and I liked it," Saun said. "But then our parents—" She did not finish the sentence, but Duffy knew that she was referring to the loss of their father and mother.

"We're going to church in the morning. Do you suppose your grandparents would let you and Ping go along?"

"I don't know. I'd like to go."

"Why don't we ask them?"

"All right, let's."

They continued walking and came to the Temple of the Ten Thousand Buddhas.

"Are there really ten thousand of these little statues here?" Juan asked.

"Actually twelve thousand eight hundred," Mr. Kerrigan said, reading from his brochure again.

By now Juan was looking shocked by all of

this. "I can't believe anybody would worship a statue like this."

"Well, you've heard the Bible stories, Juan," his father said. "You know that idol worship made a lot of trouble for the people of Israel."

Juan said, "I remember. One time they made two gold calves, and they bowed down to them."

"They sure did, and it got them into a lot of trouble," Seth said.

"Yep. When you read the Bible," Juan said, "you find out that those people always had trouble with idols."

Duffy noticed that the Li children were listening closely. "Our pastor back home said it's not right to worship a piece of clay or something carved out of wood—an idol that you can actually touch," she put in. "Because they aren't God. They're things. But then he said there are other kinds of idols, too—a kind you can't see."

Ping and Saun both stared at her. "What kind of idols do you mean? You have to be able to *see* one," said Saun.

"I don't think so," Duffy said. "An idol is anything you act as though is more important than God. You know, that was the first of the Ten Commandments—'You shall have no other gods before Me.'"

"And you're right, Duffy," Mr. Kerrigan said. "I've known people that put their business ahead of God. That meant their business was an idol."

"Yeah, and some people would rather play golf than go to church." Juan nodded wisely. "Maybe that makes golf sort of an idol."

They wandered on, looking at the thousands of statues, and Saun said, "I can see why people want to worship idols, though. My grandparents do. They want something they can see."

"I think that's true, Saun," Mr. Kerrigan said. "But remember, you can't see the real God. He doesn't have a body you can see, as we do."

"And I've heard people talk about God speaking to them," Saun said thoughtfully. "Does He ever talk to you, Mr. Kerrigan?"

"Not in the way you're talking to me. You have a body and a voice, and I can hear you with my ears. But God speaks to us inside, not with an out-loud voice. He speaks by reminding us of what His book, the Bible, says."

Ping looked very serious. "I do not understand all of this. But I have heard about Jesus. He was a good man."

"Jesus was a good man," Pearl said. "But He was more than a good man. He was God."

"But you just said that you can't see God," Saun said in some confusion. "People could see Jesus!"

"Jesus is God," Mr. Kerrigan explained. "But He was born as a baby so that He could also be a human being."

"Why would He do that?" Ping asked, his eyes wide.

"He had to become a man to die for our sins."

And then the Li children listened to Mr. Kerrigan tell why Jesus had come.

It was strange, Duffy thought, walking through a temple given over to the worship of a dead idol and at the same time to be talking about Jesus, who was alive and wanted to come into every heart.

She had felt uncomfortable entering a place with idols in it, but now that the Li children seemed so interested, she saw there had been a good purpose in coming here.

"Maybe, Dad," she whispered as they continued their walk, "maybe they'll hear enough about Jesus from us to become Christians."

"I hope so, and then I hope their grandparents will believe, too."

They stayed for a while longer at the temple. They found out such things as the name of the monk who had established it. In fact, his body was still there, encased in gold.

"That's kind of spooky," Juan said.

"Makes me feel funny, too," Seth agreed. "I don't like it."

Mr. Kerrigan asked one of the guards if he could take pictures. In China, he had learned, you must ask permission to do most things. But the guard smiled, showing the gold in his teeth. "Oh yes," he said. "Take all the pictures you want."

Juan, as usual, got bored with just walking

and looking. He began practicing his tai chi chuan.

"Juan, this is no place for that," his father said.

Juan agreed, but when his dad wasn't looking he would throw himself into a different posture and make faces.

Just before they left the temple area, they saw a strange sort of tower. It was pink.

"What's that?" asked Seth.

"It's called a *pagoda*," Mr. Kerrigan explained. "It's built as a memorial. How many stories high is it?"

The children counted quickly. "Nine!" shouted Juan.

Nearby was a huge green dog.

"Well, that ties it," Juan said. "Whoever heard of a green dog?"

As they traveled back to the city, Duffy could tell that the Li children were very interested in Jesus and not in Buddha at all.

At the Li household, Mrs. Li was waiting. She beamed at them.

"Is all ready," she said. "Come in."

They entered, and Mr. Li greeted them, bowing several times.

Juan bowed also, but then he attempted one of his tai chi chuan movements and flung his arm against a vase. It flew off the table, and only Seth's quick action saved it. He leaped out and caught the vase in midair.

Mr. Kerrigan said, "Juan, don't you do another one of those silly things in this house! Do you hear me?"

"Yes sir." Juan was very subdued for once, at least for a time.

Mrs. Li's Chinese meal was excellent.

"What is this?" Duffy asked, as Mrs. Li brought in another bowl and set it in the middle of the low table.

"Is bird nest soup," she said proudly. "Very rare."

Duffy swallowed hard. She noticed that her father was trying to look pleased.

"Bird's nest soup." He cleared his throat. "Well, I've never had that."

Pearl said, "I have. It's very good, Dad."

And, to Duffy's surprise, bird's nest soup did turn out to be very good.

Juan said, "It's better than hot dogs—maybe."

"Better than hot dog?" Mr. Li said. "Who want hot dog?"

Everyone laughed at his puzzled expression, and then Duffy explained. "It's a kind of sandwich we eat in America."

"Sandwich? What is sandwich?"

It took some time to clear the matter up, but the soup was excellent.

Afterward the kids played games while Mr. Kerrigan showed Mr. and Mrs. Li the photographs he had taken of their home. Duffy thought they acted very pleased.

Then he said, "These pictures are for you. And look—how about this?" Duffy saw him hold up an enlargement of all four of the Lis—Mr. and Mrs. Li, Saun, and Ping—grouped together in their living room.

"We find beautiful frame," Mrs. Li said. "Thank you so large."

"You're very welcome, Mrs. Li."

Before they left, Mr. Kerrigan said, "I'm taking my children to church somewhere tomorrow. I'd like very much for all of you to come."

"Oh no, we could not go out," Mrs. Li said.

"Well, then, could Saun and Ping go, perhaps?"

"If they like, yes."

"Yes! We'd like very much to go," Saun said quickly.

"Well, be ready about nine o'clock, and we'll find us a church."

The church they found was small. It met on the second floor of a warehouse and was led by an English couple, Richard and Helen Llewellen. After greeting the visitors warmly, Mr. Llewellen said, "It's good to have you visit with us. I hope you'll take part in the service."

Duffy had noticed that there were several instruments in the room, including a guitar. But it was Juan who spoke up. "I can play the guitar," he said. "And Duffy can play the piano, and Pearl there plays the drums."

"Why, you've got a regular band here! Do you play hymns?"

"We can play anything," Juan bragged. "My brother, Seth, here—he plays the bass guitar."

"I'm rather surprised that you have all these instruments," Mr. Kerrigan said.

"Well, some of our young people wanted to form a band, and they did for a while. But most of them have gone away to school now. It would be wonderful if your children could play for us. Do you play an instrument yourself, Mr. Kerrigan?"

"No, I can't even carry a tune."

"Ah, neither can I. But in any case we'd be very glad to have you take part in the service, children."

The meeting was well attended. Most of the worshipers were Chinese, but Duffy saw several black faces and a few other white visitors as well.

The pastor started the service with a prayer, and then he said, "We have a treat today—the Kerrigan family from the United States is here. And the Kerrigan youngsters have formed a band. They're going to lead our worship service."

The Li children watched with big eyes as the Kerrigan kids went to take up the instruments.

It took a few moments to get tuned up. Then Juan, who played lead guitar, said, "I'll bet you know 'Jesus Loves Me.' I heard somewhere that was the favorite hymn of China."

Many of the children grinned. "Yes. We know that," some called out.

"Then just sing along," Juan said and struck a note. They began playing, and the sound of music filled the room. Then they played hymns until finally Mr. Llewellen said, "We could listen all day, but now it's time for the sermon."

A voice of protest went up from the children, and he smiled. "Maybe we can get the Kerrigans to come back."

"Yes. Yes. Let them come back! Please come!" the cries sounded.

"I would take that as an invitation to you youngsters."

"We can come back every Sunday we're in Hong Kong, can't we, Dad?" Juan asked.

"Of course. It'll be our privilege."

The sermon was very simple. It was about Jesus being the Lamb of God. The pastor first told about the Jewish people sacrificing lambs for hundreds of years. Then he said, "The animals' blood was shed, but all of that blood never washed away one sin. But one day John the Baptist saw a man coming toward him, and he said, 'Behold, the Lamb of God who takes away the sin of the world.' That's what Jesus is—the Lamb of God that God sent to save us. When He died, His blood did pay for all our sins, and now everyone who comes to Jesus can have forgiveness."

When the sermon was coming to a close,

Duffy, who was sitting beside Saun, saw tears in the Chinese girl's eyes.

"What's wrong, Saun?"

"I need to have my sins forgiven," she whispered. "How do I do that?"

"Just pray that Jesus will forgive you," Duffy whispered back. "Tell Him that you know you've done wrong and that you want Him. Thank Him that He's already died for you. He's promised to forgive you if you ask."

And so it was that Saun Li came to Jesus that morning in a little upstairs church in Hong Kong.

"Are you going to tell your grandparents about deciding to become a Christian?" Pearl asked as they were going back to the Li house.

"Oh yes. I'll have to tell them. It wouldn't be right not to."

"Do you think they will be disappointed?"

"I do not know, but I'd like them to be forgiven, too. I know they are unhappy. They pray to the idols, but it is all nothing, really."

"Then we'll pray for them and for Ping too. That the whole family will be Christians."

When the Kerrigans had deposited the Li children at home and started back to their hotel, Juan said, "Well, this trip has been good so far, no matter what else happens."

"That's right, Juan," Duffy agreed. "Maybe God had us make this whole trip to Hong Kong just so the Lis could find Jesus."

TROUBLE
FOR JUAN

The days seemed to pass very quickly in Hong Kong. Every day the Kerrigans went to a different place for their dad to take pictures. Duffy knew he had taken hundreds of photographs. Every night he would work on the magazine story that he was writing.

But one day at breakfast he said, "We're going to do something a little different today."

"What's that, Dad?" Duffy asked.

"Not going to eat bird's nest soup again, are we?" Juan grinned.

"You didn't mind that too much," his father said quickly. "I noticed you ate your share of it. No, today we're going to try to get some good shots and a story about how a typical family lives in Hong Kong."

"I thought we'd done that with Mr. and Mrs. Li," Pearl said.

"They're not really typical," Mr. Kerrigan said, sipping his tea. "The Lis are sort of retired people and not out in the busy life of the city. What I need for this story is to find a typical couple with maybe two point three children."

"How can somebody be point three of a child?" Seth asked, a puzzled look in his eyes.

"Oh, I was just kidding. That's the average number of children people have in some places. Of course, you can't have three-tenths of a child. Anyway, I need just an ordinary couple that get up, go to work, take care of their family. I'd like to get some good shots of the kind of place they live in."

"How are we going to do that, Dad?" Seth asked. "We just can't go up and knock on somebody's door."

"That's true, so I've made some arrangements. I met a gentleman called Mr. Chiang. He's the manager of a photography store here. I've been into his shop so many times that we've become friends, and we had tea together a couple of times. I told him what I wanted to do, and he said he'd be happy to have us come and visit his home."

"It's funny how the Lord just takes care of things like that," Juan said. "You need a family and—bang—up pops a family." He turned suddenly to Seth. "Hey, Seth, did you hear about the blonde elevator operator that got fired? She forgot her route."

Everyone groaned, and Mr. Kerrigan said, "No more jokes, Juan, please. I don't think I can take it."

He paid the bill, and they left the restaurant. They got on a bus, and as they made their way along the busy streets, Duffy said, "These streets are crowded all the time. Somebody said there are people all over even late at night."

"It would drive American drivers crazy, wouldn't it?" Mr. Kerrigan said. "When I get caught in a traffic jam, I know it really irritates me."

They kept looking out at the busy street until finally the bus came to the stop he wanted.

"That's it across the street. The Peninsula Hotel."

"It's a skyscraper," Duffy said as they got off the bus. "Are there offices in this building?"

"No. Nothing but apartments."

"Wow, that thing must be fifty stories tall," Seth said.

"No, it's thirty, but it contains over a thousand apartments. Mr. Chiang says nearly four thousand people live in this one building."

They went inside and got on the elevator. Mr. Kerrigan punched a button. They got off at the twenty-second floor and went down a long hall. Duffy thought the place looked like a huge motel. They passed a small group of young people who were headed down the hall laughing and talking. They greeted the Kerrigans happily as they went by.

When they got to Apartment 2208, Mr. Kerrigan knocked, and the door opened almost at once. A Chinese lady wearing stylish clothes that could have been bought in America smiled at them.

"You must be Mr. Kerrigan."

"Yes, I am. Are you Mrs. Chiang?"

"Yes. My husband will be here in just a moment. He's getting ready for work. Won't you come in?"

The family entered, and Mr. Kerrigan introduced the youngsters.

Mrs. Chiang said, "And these are our children, Richard and Lotus. Richard's eight, and Lotus is six."

The Chiang children bowed politely, then said in perfect English, "How do you do?"

"They speak English very well," Mr. Kerrigan said.

"Oh yes. Most people learn English in school here, but we also get American programs, so we practice our English all the time."

At that moment Mr. Chiang came in. He was wearing a dark blue suit with a white shirt and a maroon tie. "Well, Mr. Kerrigan," he said. "I'm glad to see you."

"Thank you, Mr. Chiang. As you see, I'm taking you up on your offer."

"Well, get your camera out. I'm ready to be photographed. I've put on my best suit. My wife's wearing her best dress."

"We've got on our best clothes, too," Richard said.

"Is our picture going to be in a magazine?" Lotus asked curiously.

"It sure will be, and I'm going to send you all copies of it so you can impress your friends."

"Well, let me show you around," Mr. Chiang said. "You may take whatever pictures you would like."

"Not many ladies would let a herd of strangers like us come in and take pictures. I sure appreciate this, Mrs. Chiang."

"Oh, it is nothing. I try to keep the house presentable."

Mrs. Chiang showed the children the apartment. It was very, very small—much smaller than most houses in the States. It had a single window in the living room. It had two tiny bedrooms, a kitchen nook, and a bathroom.

Duffy was shocked, and she whispered to Seth when she had a chance, "This is so small! I wouldn't want to live in a place like this. Never!"

"*Shh.* They're very proud of their house," Seth whispered back. "Besides, where I came from in Nigeria, this would be a palace to many people."

The visit proved to be helpful, indeed. Mr. Kerrigan took pictures of the Chiangs, and, of course, it did not take long to photograph the apartment. They talked for a while and then got ready to leave.

"Thank you very much, Mr. and Mrs. Chiang. I'll be sure to send you pictures when the magazine comes out."

"Come any time. We will always be glad to see you."

As they went down on the elevator, Duffy said, "They're such nice people."

"Yes, they are," Mr. Kerrigan said. "And just thinking about their living in that tiny apartment makes me feel ungrateful. We have that big, nice house at home with lots of room to roam around. In the States we forget how blessed we are by God. We just take for granted things like nice houses and indoor plumbing."

"I know. I remember when we were in Africa. I would have given anything for a nice indoor bathroom," Duffy said. "And now I don't even think about having one."

"Well, any more pictures to take today, Dad?"

"Yes, Pearl. We're going to spend all afternoon at the Sung Dynasty Village."

"What's *that*?" she asked curiously.

"It's kind of a living museum. You remember when we went to Plymouth Village in Massachusetts—the place where a village had been built looking exactly like the ones the Pilgrims lived in?"

"Oh yes! That was fun. The people all wore costumes, and they all pretended to be real Pilgrims."

"Well, this is the same kind of thing. Only it's a living museum of the Sung Dynasty—a Chinese family in power a long time ago. I think you'll find it interesting."

The Kerrigans got off the bus when it reached the Sung Dynasty Village. Right away Juan cried, "Get your camera out, Dad! This is going to be real fun. See? They're wearing old-time clothes just like in the history books."

Duffy too stood staring at the village people. All were wearing not modern clothes but ancient Chinese dress.

"I wonder if any of these women had their feet bound," Seth said.

"What are you talking about?" Juan asked.

"Don't you remember that? We learned that in school."

"I was thinking of something else that day. Why would anybody bind up their feet?"

"Back in the old days, the Chinese thought the sign of a pretty woman was how small her feet were. So when they were just babies they would tie their feet up so tight that they couldn't grow."

"How cruel!" Duffy said. "I know it must have hurt."

"It did," her father said. "It was very painful.

Nobody does that anymore, of course, but the ladies in those days wound up with feet kind of like a hoof rather than a real foot."

Duffy shivered. "That's awful! Why would anyone think that deformed feet are beautiful?"

"It doesn't sound beautiful to me," Juan said. "I read once that in some places people think the prettiest thing about a girl is the back of her neck." He nudged Duffy. "They wouldn't like yours. It's always dirty."

"It is not!" Duffy cried, shoving him away. "You say such awful things!"

The two continued to wrangle until they got inside the village. There they stopped arguing to watch a craftsman make incense. Another man, at a stand right next door, was making beautiful, delicate umbrellas. Duffy said, "I've just got to have one of those! A handmade umbrella."

"You'd probably never get it home," Seth said. "They're so fragile."

"I'll buy a tube and ship it home. Can I do that, Dad?"

"I think that would be nice. All of us need to buy something to remember this trip by."

The most fascinating thing for Juan seemed to be the vendor that sold candy. He was making it at a cart with a small stove, and Juan bought some. "This is great!" he cried. "I'm going to buy enough of it to last me our whole trip."

"No, you're not! You eat enough as it is," his father said.

They wandered farther along the streets and stopped for some time at an acrobat show.

"The Chinese are famous acrobats," Mr. Kerrigan said. "Some of the best acrobats in the world are Chinese."

"You remember when we went to the circus?" Seth exclaimed. "There was a whole troupe of Chinese acrobats. They were good!"

By the time the tour was almost over, Mr. Kerrigan had used up ten rolls of film.

Duffy and Pearl both liked the traditional wedding that was put on. The bride wore a red wedding dress. Although it was done in the Chinese language—which Pearl understood a little of—Duffy enjoyed it even not understanding a word.

But Juan said, "Ah, this is goofy. Let's find something better." He looked around and said, "There! Now that's what I want to see."

It was a kung fu exhibition. Men were going through their martial arts exercises, and Juan, of course, had to go up to one and say, "If you need any advice, maybe I can help you."

The Chinese, who was wearing a white kung fu outfit, grinned and said, "You're an expert, are you?"

"Well, I'm going to be."

"Good for you, but it takes a lot of work and years of practice."

"Not for me. I've got a handle on it."

"Would you care to give me a little sample?"

Duffy knew Juan had not expected this. He looked over at his dad and said, "I don't expect you'd want me to do that, would you, Dad?"

Their father, however, had caught the smile from the Chinese expert. "Why, I think you should give everybody an exhibition, but don't hurt that man. After all, he's only three times as big as you are."

A crowd had gathered around, some Americans and some British, and they all began to smile.

"Go ahead," Mr. Kerrigan said. "Throw him up in the air. Show him how it's done, Juan."

"Do it, Juan," Duffy teased. "But, as Dad said, don't hurt him. I mean, after all, you're such a terror that everyone in America is scared when you walk by."

She could tell that Juan would like to have gotten out of it, but there was no hope. The martial arts expert pulled him to the center of the ring and said, "All right. Let us begin." The man in front of him looked very dangerous!

"As you know, first we bow like this," the expert said. He bowed.

Juan bowed.

"And now we will begin."

Juan knew one thing about kung fu—often the kung fu experts would leap in the air and kick at their opponents. Desperately he jumped up and made a wild kick. But his ankles were suddenly caught in two steely vises, and he found himself hanging upside down.

By now everyone was laughing.

"Let me down!" Juan cried. "Let me down!"

Gently the man lowered Juan and said, "I think you need a few more lessons. Come back when you are a few years older."

Juan scrambled to his feet, looked around at the people laughing, and then turned to the kung fu artist. He bowed and said, "I let you off easy this time, but you'd better watch it."

As they left the village, Duffy said, "I'm glad you didn't hurt that man, Juan."

Juan reached over and pinched Duffy. "You'd better be careful, or I'll give you some of what I gave him."

10

A NIGHT AT
THE LI HOUSE

I've got a little problem," Mr. Kerrigan said.

The Kerrigans were all sitting around on the floor, where they had been having their nightly Bible time. There were not enough chairs for everyone, so they had decided at the very beginning just to sit on the floor while they had their prayer time together.

"What's the matter, Dad?" Seth asked. "Is it a real big problem?"

"Oh no. But I need to make an overnight trip, and I don't know what to do with all of you."

"Couldn't we go along?" Pearl said.

"Not this time. I'm going with another photographer, and we're making a short flight in a small plane. So I have this opportunity for some photo taking, but I can't leave you here alone."

"I know what we can do!" Duffy said.

"I know, too," Juan said. "We can take care of ourselves. You don't have to worry about us."

"No. I won't leave you all here alone, Juan. That wouldn't be proper. What's your idea, Duffy?"

"Well, Ping and Saun asked us just yesterday if we could come and spend the night with them sometime. Maybe we could do that while you're gone."

"But there's no place for you to stay, is there? I mean, their home is very small."

"Oh, that won't be any problem. We'll just take some covers and sleep on the floor. It'll be just like a sleepover."

"Well, I don't know about all of this," Mr. Kerrigan said. "Older people sometimes don't like having a bunch of yelling children around."

"That's right," Juan said. "If we do this, you'll have to stop all your yelling, Duffy. And you too, Pearl. You're gonna have to learn to behave like Seth and me." He nodded at his father. "You know how girls are, Dad—always making a big racket."

"Oh, you hush, Juan!" Pearl said, for once not pleased with Juan's teasing. "You're the one that makes most of the noise when we go anywhere."

"Anyway," Mr. Kerrigan continued, "I'm still not sure the Lis would be able to cope with four more active youngsters."

"But it was their idea, Dad," Duffy said. "They

told Ping and Saun it would be nice if we could come and spend one whole night with them."

"Well, that would certainly take care of the problem." He pushed his fingers through his hair. "So what do you think? Would you all like to do that —after I check with the Lis?"

"Oh sure, Dad," Seth said. "I like Mr. and Mrs. Li a lot. They're nice people."

"It's all right with me, and it would solve my problem. We'll see if it can be worked out."

And so it was that the next morning after breakfast, Mr. Kerrigan took the children to the Li house. Mrs. Li and Ping and Saun all met them at the door.

As they stepped inside, Mr. Kerrigan said, smiling, "Mrs. Li, are you still sure you want to do this? Children can be awfully noisy and a lot of trouble."

"Ah, no trouble." Mrs. Li smiled, too, and bobbed her head several times. "Be good for Ping and Saun, and we will be most honored."

"Yes," Mr. Li agreed, entering from the bedroom. "We be most happy."

"Your English is getting very good, Mr. Li," Mr. Kerrigan said.

"Yes. Good English." Mr. Li fairly beamed.

"Well, I'll leave them with you. If they need any discipline from me, just write it down, and I'll take care of it."

"You don't have to worry, Dad. I'll see that everybody behaves," Juan promised.

"I'm sure you will, Juan."

After he left, Saun said, "There's a playground not far from here. They play soccer and all kinds of things there. If it is all right with you, Grandmother and Grandfather, we will go."

"Yes. You go have good time."

The well-equipped playground, only a few blocks away, was already filled with children. They spent all morning there and went back to the Li house at noon. Mrs. Li had fixed a snack, and Saun said, "After we have a nap, we will make a fine dinner for you, won't we, Grandmother?"

"Yes. You girls will help."

"And you will come with me," Mr. Li said, nodding at the boys.

"Where are we going, Mr. Li?"

"I take you to wharf. You see fishing boats. Maybe catch fish."

"Ooh, that'll be cool," Juan said. "I'm a good fisherman."

So, later in the day, when Mr. Li took the boys off to the wharf, Duffy and Pearl began getting a lesson in Chinese cooking.

Under Mrs. Li's teaching they helped make spicy hot soup with noodles. They helped prepare chicken with walnut and black bean sauce. They helped with the rice and onion cakes and Juan's favorite—shrimp egg rolls. They worked on preparing dinner the rest of the afternoon, and by the time Mr. Li and the boys came back—starved, Juan said—the food was almost ready.

Duffy whispered to Juan before the meal, "Now, Juan, show some good manners."

"Who, me? I always show good manners."

To her surprise, Juan did exhibit good manners. Duffy kept watching for him to stuff his mouth so that his cheeks bulged out, but he ate very politely indeed. He told the girls what they had seen at the wharf and that Mr. Li was going to take them back for a ride on one of the fishing boats. One of his cousins owned it.

After dinner, the girls insisted on cleaning up. Then they all sat in the living room, and Mr. and Mrs. Li talked about their early life in China.

Much of it had to be translated by Ping or Saun, but it was very interesting. After a time, Mrs. Li brought out pictures of their family. They had two sons, but both lived in mainland China with their families. The Lis seemed very proud of them and said that they were coming soon for a visit.

Duffy noticed that the discomfort there had been between the grandparents and their grandchildren seemed to have gone away, and she was very happy about that.

The sleeping arrangements were simple. The girls took Saun's room, and the boys made a bed on the floor in the combination living room-dining room-kitchen. Before anyone went to sleep, however, Duffy said, "We always have a Bible reading and prayer time before we go to bed. Would you like to join us?"

Saun and Ping wanted to, but then Mr. and Mrs. Li also came in and sat down. Duffy explained what they were going to do, and both Lis smiled and said, "Yes."

It was Pearl's turn to choose a Scripture, and she chose the Twenty-third Psalm. It was her favorite, and she read it first in English. Then she said, "I learned it in Chinese a long time ago—when I was at the orphanage. I will say that too."

None of the other Kerrigans understood the Twenty-third Psalm in Chinese, but Duffy thought it sounded very pretty. She also saw that Mr. and Mrs. Li were listening intently. She knew Saun had told her grandparents that she had become a Christian, and Duffy had been afraid they would be offended. But she saw they were not. They finished listening to the psalm, and then Mrs. Li said, "Very beautiful."

Mr. Li did not say anything, but he too listened as the children talked for a while about how Jesus takes care of His people as a good shepherd cares for his sheep. Then each Kerrigan prayed—for their father and their friends at home and then that the Li family would be especially blessed by God.

When the amen was said, Mr. Li said, "Very good. Thank you." He got up and left the room, and Mrs. Li soon followed him.

"They don't seem upset because you've become a Christian, Saun."

"They are interested in Jesus. My grandfather has a Bible that some missionary gave him a long time ago. He never read it before, but I see him reading it now."

"I believe your whole family's going to be saved because of you, Saun," Duffy said.

Pearl said. "We're going to pray for that."

Saun Li took the hands of both girls. "I want my whole family to know Jesus."

And Duffy was sure she knew why God had brought the Kerrigans to Hong Kong.

THE
SHOPPING TRIP

I think it's time we finish buying whatever we want to take home with us," Mr. Kerrigan said one morning. "How would you kids like to go shopping?"

"Yes, yes, yes!" Duffy cried. "I've been saving up all my money, and I want to get a little something for each of my friends."

"Well, the Western District of Hong Kong is where most of the shopping for tourists takes place. So I think we'll go there this afternoon."

"Can Saun and Ping go with us?" Pearl asked quickly.

"I don't see why not. They've been with you kids almost every day."

"Dad, it's wonderful how much happier they

are now," Duffy said. "Do you remember how scared Saun and Ping were when they first came?"

"I remember, and they do seem much happier now," Mr. Kerrigan said. "Also, Mrs. Li just told me that one of their sons is coming to live in Hong Kong. He has three children. That will give Saun and Ping some more family here. I think the son is coming mostly to take care of his parents. They're getting on in years, and they need some family support."

"One thing about the Chinese," Seth said, "they like their families."

"That's right," his father said. "Family life is very strong in China."

"If we're going shopping, I may have to get a little loan from you, Dad," Juan said. "I don't have quite enough money to buy all I want to."

"What did you do with all your money? I gave you all the same amount to spend."

"Well, I had some . . . expenses."

"He ate it up. That's what he did," Pearl said. "He spends more money on food than the rest of us put together."

"Well, I'm a growing boy."

"Don't you think we're growing?" Seth asked.

"You're not getting any more money, Juan. If you chose to eat up your spending money, that's your business. You've got to learn responsibility."

Juan protested, but he did not get anywhere

with his father. Mr. Kerrigan was a kind and gentle man, but he was also very firm.

That afternoon the Kerrigans went to pick up Saun and Ping for their shopping trip. Duffy was surprised to find Mr. and Mrs. Li dressed up and ready to go.

"We go, too." Mr. Li smiled, bowing and nodding as he always did.

"Why, that's fine, Mr. Li. We'll have a great time."

"I think that's good, Saun," Duffy whispered. "Your grandparents need to get out of the apartment."

"Now that my uncle and aunt are coming, I think they'll go out a lot more."

The Western District was reached by riding one of the double-decker buses again. The older Lis sat on the lower deck along with Mr. Kerrigan, but the youngsters raced to the top, as always. There was something exciting about being above everybody else. All around them on the top deck were other youngsters, laughing and singing songs in Chinese. Sometimes Ping and Saun joined in.

"That's what I liked about those buses in England. They were two-deckers like this. You can see everything," Pearl said to Saun.

"It is fun." Then Saun said, "I'm so glad my grandparents wanted to come along. They hardly ever go anywhere."

"Well, that will all change when your uncle and aunt get here," Duffy told her. "And then you'll have cousins to play with and go places with. Just wait."

Ping was sitting close to Seth, as he always did when he had a chance. "Seth, I'm glad you and your family came to Hong Kong when you did."

"So am I." Seth had grown very fond of the younger boy, and he patted him on the shoulder. "You're going to do fine."

"Saun and I were so scared when we came. We didn't really know our grandparents."

"Well, you know them now, and they're nice people. They love you a lot."

"And my uncle and aunt are coming. Did I tell you?"

"I heard."

"I don't remember them, but Grandfather and Grandmother say we'll like our cousins a lot. They're about our age, so we'll have someone to talk to and do things with."

"I'm real glad for you, Ping. And you'll have to write to me, and I'll write back to you."

"I will. I promise."

"Writing's not quite as good as being with someone, but when you're separated by an ocean, it's the next best thing."

Thousands of people, it seemed, were thronging the streets in the Western District. It was hard to get through the crowds, and Mr. Kerrigan said,

"Let's all stay close together. If anybody gets lost, you all have Mr. Li's telephone number and our hotel number sewed into your clothes, don't you?"

"Sure," Juan said. "I sewed mine right to my underwear. In case I lose my shirt, I still got it."

"Well, I hope you won't do anything like that."

Duffy grinned. "So do I. He's probably not wearing clean underwear."

Juan started to argue about this and offered to take off his shirt and show her.

But Seth said, "I don't think you'd better do that. It might be against the law in Hong Kong to take off your shirt in public."

They kept wandering through the packed streets. In one place, shop owners sold all kinds of cloth. Some were extravagant silks in beautiful, bright reds, oranges, blues, and yellows. They began to buy inexpensive souvenirs for their friends at home.

Juan wished he had saved more of his spending money. All at once he cried, "Look, there's a snake! I want one of those."

"You're *not* bringing a snake home with you," his father said quickly.

"It's just a dried snake."

"What do you want with a dried snake?" Seth asked.

"Well, nobody else has one. I thought somebody in the family ought to have a dried snake."

Mr. and Mrs. Li seemed to be enjoying themselves. The others moved along very slowly so that they would not have any trouble keeping up. Finally they came to an herbal shop, and Mrs. Li began to make purchases.

"Wow, your grandmother sure likes herbs," Seth said to Ping.

"For a long time that was all that people in China had for medicine, and Grandmother still thinks they're good for you."

"Lots of people in America do, too. I don't know much about them myself."

One thing that amused Juan was the way that Mrs. Li haggled with the vendors. The owner of the herbal shop would give her a price, and her eyes would open wide. "No! Too much!" she would say, then fly off into a long speech in Chinese.

Juan thought this arguing was funny. He said to Duffy, "That's the way we ought to bargain for stuff. I'm going to do the same thing."

Juan tried bargaining when he saw a tiny carved buffalo that he liked very much. In fact, he got into a terrific argument with the man who ran the stall and succeeded only in making him mad.

Mrs. Li stepped in then and spoke quietly to the man in Chinese. He calmed down but muttered something.

"What did he say?" Juan demanded.

Saun giggled. "He said you were a wild buffalo yourself."

Mrs. Li bought the buffalo at a reduced price and handed it to Juan. "It is a gift," she said.

"Ah, you didn't have to do that, Mrs. Li."

But it turned out that Mr. and Mrs. Li bought gifts for all of the Kerrigan children that day.

Sitting on top of the double-decker on the way home, the kids decided to sing. Juan wanted to sing "The Star Spangled Banner," but the others said that was too hard, so they sang "On Top of Old Smokey." Juan was surprised to see that some of the other tourists knew that song. Some were Americans, of course. But soon the whole crowd was singing "On Top of Old Smokey." It looked as if some riders were singing in Chinese, which Juan found very funny.

They delivered the Lis to their home and then went on back to the hotel with their packages.

"I think we'll box these up and ship them instead of trying to carry them on the plane. Some of them are very delicate," Mr. Kerrigan said.

"We'll help you, Dad," Seth said. "We can get some packing boxes in the morning. I know where they sell stuff like that."

Pearl said, "It's funny, but I sort of hate to go home."

"It's been good to be here," Duffy agreed. "I'm so happy about the Lis. I know one reason the Lord sent us to Hong Kong was to help them learn to live together. But the most important reason was to introduce the whole family to Jesus."

"The Lord is wise. He sends His people where He wants to use them," their dad said.

"In the Bible He sent angels sometimes," Juan said. "For all you know," he teased, "I may be an angel myself."

With a laugh, Mr. Kerrigan grabbed Juan and wrestled him to the floor. "You are no angel," he said.

Juan struggled and shouted. The rest of the children piled on. Trying to put their father down was a game they often played at home. He was gentle with them but was strong, so they didn't succeed.

However, they made so much racket that finally an angry knock came at the door. It was the man from the next room. He said crossly, "Noise. Too much noise."

"I'm sorry. My children and I were just playing."

"You too old to play with children," the man scolded.

"No," Mr. Kerrigan said. "I'll never get too old to play with my children."

HEADING HOME

I love getting ready to go places," Duffy said as she packed her suitcase, "but I hate getting ready to go home."

"Me too," Pearl agreed. "When you're getting ready to go, the fun all lies out ahead of you. But going back, the fun's over."

As the girls continued to pack their things, Pearl said, "And sometimes planning a vacation is better than the vacation itself."

"That's right. You remember when we were going to Disneyland? We planned going for months, and when we got there it rained every day, and you and I got sick."

"I remember. It was fun to plan it, but the trip itself wasn't so good."

By the time the two girls finished packing,

their father was knocking on their hotel door. "Time to leave, girls. Are you ready?" he asked, when Duffy let him in.

"All packed. Did you check Juan's suitcase?" she asked.

"Yes, and I made him do it all over again. He just stuffed things in there. His suitcase looked like a big, ugly, purple balloon. Those awful colors he chose for his suitcases, anyway—purple and orange!"

"Well," Duffy said, "he says it makes them easier to keep up with."

"It does that. You can see them a mile away," Mr. Kerrigan complained.

They put the girls' suitcases on the hotel cart and then pushed it to where they added Mr. Kerrigan's bags. After that they knocked on the boys' door.

Juan opened it, announcing, "All ready."

"Let me see that suitcase."

"Here it is," Juan said proudly.

Mr. Kerrigan stared at it sadly. It still was lumpy. "Well, if you've got everything in there, I guess that's the best you can do. I hope customs doesn't make you unload it."

"How about mine, Dad?" Seth asked.

Seth's suitcases were always neat. "They look as good as usual, son. You're the best packer in the crew, I think."

"I wish we could have stayed longer," Juan

said. "I would have been a champion at tai chi chuan if we could have stayed another month." He began spinning around the room.

Mr. Kerrigan sighed. "It's a good thing you can play a guitar well, because you sure can't do tai chi chuan. You look absolutely silly."

"Are we going to stop off at the Li house to say good-bye?" Pearl asked.

"I promised them we would. We can't stay long, though. We're taking a taxi this time, so we'll just ask him to wait."

It was a chore to get all the luggage in the taxi. As a matter of fact, the cab driver had to tie some of it on the top. But they were all packed in at last and drove to the Li household.

The Lis were all waiting for them.

"We can stay only a minute," Mr. Kerrigan said. "We're on our way to the airport."

Mr. and Mrs. Li both bowed, and Mrs. Li said with tears in her eyes, "I hate you go home. You very good for us."

Mr. Li bowed again. "Thank you much. We miss you big."

It was a sad parting. The girls were all trying to keep from crying, and even Juan, tough as he was, had to bite his lip as he said good-bye. He even went around and shook hands with everyone.

Mrs. Li hugged him. "You good boy," she said. "Take care of you brother and sisters."

"You see, Mrs. Li knows who takes care of everything," Juan said to cover his embarrassment.

"I'll be sending you copies of the magazine when it comes out," Mr. Kerrigan promised again. "It'll be a while—maybe six months. But we'll be writing to you before that."

"Thank you much. You good man. Have good family," Mr. Li said.

The girls were still having a hard time with their farewells. "You will have to come back to America and see us sometime," Duffy said to Saun.

"Do that," Seth said to Ping and gave him a hug around his shoulders. "Next time I see you, you'll be as big as I am."

Finally the good-byes were over, and the Kerrigans went out and got in the taxi. As they left, they waved out the windows.

Duffy said, "I hate good-byes."

"So do I," Pearl said. She wiped her eyes. "I can't help crying a little bit."

"Well, kids, God has given us a good trip," their dad said. "I got some great pictures, and I think the story will go well. But I agree that the best thing that came out of it was what happened to Saun and in the Li family. By the way, do you remember the Bible story we read just before we left?"

"About the Good Samaritan?" Pearl said.

"That's the one. Well, you kids were Good

Samaritans to the Lis. Now we'll keep on praying until Ping and Mr. and Mrs. Li become believers, too."

After a long silence, Juan piped up. "I'm glad we got to come. I like Ping and Saun. And Mr. and Mrs. Li are OK people. The only thing not so good is I didn't get to go back to the Sung Dynasty Village and show that kung fu expert what I could really do."

"We might have some extra time before we need to be at the airport," his father said. "Why don't we drive by the Village on the way? You can show him how it's really done."

Juan stared at his father. "Uh . . . no," he said quickly, "I don't think we have time."

"Sure, we've got time. I'd like to see you beat him," Seth said.

Everyone began to laugh then, and Juan felt his face grow red. "You're just making fun of me."

Duffy gave him a hug. "Never mind. You're more fun than anyone I know, Juan."

Seth thumped his brother on the shoulder. "More fun but not much good at kung fu."

Get swept away in the many Gilbert Morris Adventures available from Moody Press:

"Too Smart" Jones

4025-8 Pool Party Thief
4026-6 Buried Jewels
4027-4 Disappearing Dogs
4028-2 Dangerous Woman
4029-0 Stranger in the Cave
4030-4 Cat's Secret
4031-2 Stolen Bicycle
4032-0 Wilderness Mystery
4033-9 Spooky Mansion
4034-7 Mysterious Artist

Come along for the adventures and mysteries Juliet "Too Smart" Jones always manages to find. She and her other homeschool friends solve these great adventures and learn biblical truths along the way. Ages 9-14

Seven Sleepers - The Lost Chronicles

3667-6 The Spell of the Crystal Chair
3668-4 The Savage Game of Lord Zarak
3669-2 The Strange Creatures of Dr. Korbo
3670-6 City of the Cyborgs
3671-4 The Temptations of Pleasure Island
3672-2 Victims of Nimbo
3673-0 The Terrible Beast of Zor

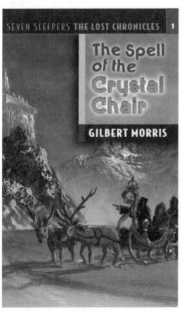

More exciting adventures from the Seven Sleepers. As these exciting young people attempt to faithfully follow Goél, they learn important moral and spiritual lessons. Come along with them as they encounter danger, intrigue, and mystery. Ages 10-14

Dixie Morris Animal Adventures

3363-4 Dixie and Jumbo
3364-2 Dixie and Stripes
3365-0 Dixie and Dolly
3366-9 Dixie and Sandy
3367-7 Dixie and Ivan
3368-5 Dixie and Bandit
3369-3 Dixie and Champ
3370-7 Dixie and Perry
3371-5 Dixie and Blizzard
3382-3 Dixie and Flash

Follow the exciting adventures of this animal lover as she learns more of God and His character through her many adventures underneath the Big Top.
Ages 9-14

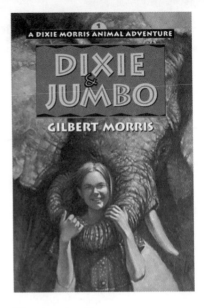

The Daystar Voyages

4102-X Secret of the Planet Makon
4106-8 Wizards of the Galaxy
4107-6 Escape From the Red Comet
4108-4 Dark Spell Over Morlandria
4109-2 Revenge of the Space Pirates
4110-6 Invasion of the Killer Locusts
4111-4 Dangers of the Rainbow Nebula
4112-2 The Frozen Space Pilot
4113-0 White Dragon of Sharnu
4114-9 Attack of the Denebian Starship

Join the crew of the Daystar as they traverse the wide expanse of space. Adventure and danger abound, but they learn time and again that God is truly the Master of the Universe.
Ages 10-14

MOODY
The Name You Can Trust
1-800-678-8812 www.MoodyPress.org

Seven Sleepers Series

3681-1 Flight of the Eagles
3682-X The Gates of Neptune
3683-3 The Swords of Camelot
3684-6 The Caves That Time Forgot
3685-4 Winged Riders of the Desert
3686-2 Empress of the Underworld
3687-0 Voyage of the Dolphin
3691-9 Attack of the Amazons
3692-7 Escape with the Dream Maker
3693-5 The Final Kingdom

Go with Josh and his friends as they are sent by Goél, their spiritual leader, on dangerous and challenging voyages to conquer the forces of darkness in the new world. Ages 10-14

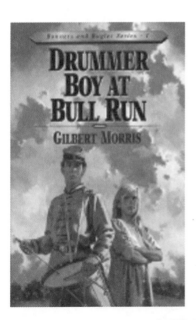

Bonnets and Bugles Series

0911-3 Drummer Boy at Bull Run
0912-1 Yankee Belles in Dixie
0913-X The Secret of Richmond Manor
0914-8 The Soldier Boy's Discovery
0915-6 Blockade Runner
0916-4 The Gallant Boys of Gettysburg
0917-2 The Battle of Lookout Mountain
0918-0 Encounter at Cold Harbor
0919-9 Fire Over Atlanta
0920-2 Bring the Boys Home

Follow good friends Leah Carter and Jeff Majors as they experience danger, intrigue, compassion, and love in these civil war adventures. Ages 10-14

MOODY
The Name You Can Trust
1-800-678-8812 www.MoodyPress.org